Secrets

PLAIN AND SIMPLE

Courage is something you can never lose, because courage is something you can always choose.

—An Amish Proverb

Sugarcreek Amish Mysteries

Secrets
PLAIN AND SIMPLE

ELIZABETH LUDWIG

Guideposts

New York

Cover and interior design by Müllerhaus
Cover illustration by Bill Bruning, represented by Deborah Wolfe, LTD.
Typeset by Aptara, Inc.

Printed and bound in the United States of America
10 9 8 7 6 5 4 3

To Susan Downs:
I never could have guessed what God would have in store when He started me on this publishing journey. Thankfully, He put people in my path who believed in me and encouraged me through all the ups and downs. You are one of those. I am blessed to call you friend.

Chapter One

Cheryl wiped the last bit of mashed sweet potato from little Rebecca's chin and then planted a noisy kiss on her rosy cheek.

"There you go, Boo. All clean."

In response, Rebecca cooed and raised her arms to be lifted from her high chair. Cheryl laughingly obliged. No sooner had the little girl's feet hit the floor than she was off, chasing the cat up onto the counter and then higher, onto the refrigerator, where he stared down at the baby with disdain, the tip of his tail flicking with irritation.

"Oh, come now, Beau," Cheryl chided, dumping Rebecca's dish and sippy cup in the sink. "She only pulls on your ears *sometimes*. It's her way of saying she loves you."

Beau stared, his crystal-blue eyes unblinking.

Cheryl propped her hands on her hips. "What? She pulls my ears too. You don't see me complaining."

Done with the conversation, Beau dipped his head and began licking his paw. Cheryl smiled. For a Siamese, Beau was remarkably patient with the baby. He never scratched when he was irritated, just made for higher ground, a happy compromise that Cheryl willingly obliged in order to keep them both happy.

Spying one of the blocks Levi had made for her under the table, Rebecca wiggled after it and plopped herself down, content to make a game of banging it against a chair leg. Cheryl pushed a lock of hair from her forehead wearily. Maybe Rebecca would stay occupied long enough for her to finish washing the pile of dishes in the sink, or hanging the laundry on the line, or sweeping the floor...

She sighed as her foot crunched on another Cheerio. It seemed there were never enough hours in the day anymore, even with her staying home now to care for the baby. She lifted Levi's jacket from the back of a chair and pressed it to her nose for a long sniff before depositing it on a hook next to the door. She might be busy, but she wouldn't trade a second of her life for anything in the world. Who would have thought that being a wife and mother could fill her heart so?

Naomi would, of course.

She smiled as her friend's familiar face appeared at the kitchen door. Giving a wave, Naomi entered without knocking, an Amish practice that had taken Cheryl aback at first, but which she didn't give a second thought to now.

"*Guder mariye,*" Cheryl said, the Pennsylvania Dutch greeting as familiar to her now as her southern momma's way of drawling "mornin', y'all."

"Guder mariye." Naomi placed a basket on the counter, gave Cheryl a hug, and then crossed to the table and bent to peek underneath. "Where is that sweet *boppli?* Rebecca?" She stuck out her hands to the child. "Come and give your *Oma* a hug."

Rebecca needed no further prompting. Letting out a squeal, she scrambled from under the table straight into Naomi's waiting arms.

"Ah, there you are. Oma has been waiting all morning to see you."

Patting Naomi's cheeks, Rebecca cooed, "Oma, Oma," over and over, her delight obvious.

Tilting to rest her forehead against Rebecca's, Naomi whispered something in Pennsylvania Dutch, to which Rebecca replied, *"Ja."*

"Goot. Then come and see." Taking Rebecca by the hand, Naomi led her to the basket, lowered it off the counter, then pulled back the checkered cloth on top. "See anything you like?"

"Cookie!" Rebecca said, clapping her hands together before snatching one off the top and taking a greedy bite. It was one of the few words she knew, but one she used often, thanks to her indulgent grandmother.

Laughing, Naomi replaced the basket on the counter. "There are more cookies in there for you and Levi. Snickerdoodles, your favorite," she said, turning to Cheryl.

Cheryl shook her head and laughed. "How will I ever stick to my diet with you constantly plying me with cookies?"

Naomi crossed her arms and looked her over teasingly. "What diet? You are slimmer now than before you had Rebecca."

Cheryl hid a pleased smile. It was true. Running after the baby and working from home had done wonders for her waistline. Lately, she'd had no trouble keeping off that extra five pounds that had plagued her before she and Levi married, even with Naomi's home cooking.

"There is also more homemade baby food in the basket," Naomi said, pulling one of the jars out and setting it on the counter. "I wanted to get one last batch made before we get too busy with the farm."

Homemade baby food was one of the many, *many* benefits of having an Amish mother-in-law. Cheryl lifted another jar from the basket gratefully. "Naomi, you know Rebecca is eating a lot of solid food. You didn't have to go through so much work."

"It is not work when it brings so much joy." She bent to wipe the cookie crumbs from Rebecca's cheeks and hands. "To the giver as well as the *givee*, ain't so?"

She smiled and chucked Rebecca under the chin. Puckering up, she accepted a wet kiss and then sighed happily as the baby tottered around, her chubby legs unsteady.

Watching them, Cheryl's heart swelled with joy. What a blessing to have a woman who was not only her mother-in-law and grandmother to her daughter but also her friend!

Blinking away tears of gratitude, Cheryl turned on the tap and ran warm water over the dishes in the sink. "So, what do you have planned today?"

Naomi picked up Rebecca's block and took turns handing it to her and then taking it back. "I meant to go by the Swiss Miss. I have several things Esther asked me to bring to the store, but now I am not sure I will have time. Seth asked me to stop by the feedstore and pick up some supplies for the petting zoo."

"Esther's restocking already? Didn't you just make a delivery Thursday?"

Naomi's head bobbed. "Ja, but Esther ran a special on homemade breads this week. She gave away a sample jar of jam to anyone who bought two or more loaves. They sold so well, she is all out of strawberry *and* blackberry."

"Wow." Cheryl scrubbed absently at a dinner plate while she thought over Naomi's words. "Esther is doing really well at the store. She really has a head for business."

"Ja, this is true. Seth even said he will have to ask her for some tips for the petting zoo and the corn maze." She laughed and shook her head at Rebecca, making her giggle. "As if we need more business. As it is, I can hardly keep up."

Waving her bonnet strings at Rebecca, Naomi clucked her tongue and then clapped her hands, coaxing her closer until she was near enough to hug. "*Ach*, if only they could stay this little forever. Instead they grow up and give their mommas headaches worrying about them."

Cheryl looked up from the sink full of soapy water. Seth and Naomi had several children, but Esther was the youngest. Luckily, she was sweet natured and kind, even if she was a tad headstrong. "Worrying? Not about Esther, I hope?"

Naomi shrugged but said nothing more. She reluctantly pried herself away from playing with Rebecca and flicked her fingers over her apron to smooth out the wrinkles. "Well, I should be going. Even if I hurry, I will be late getting home to make supper."

Cheryl dried her hands on a towel then motioned toward the door. "Do you have the things for Esther with you now?"

"Ja, they are in the buggy."

"Well, why don't you let me take them?"

Naomi frowned uncertainly. "Cheryl, are you sure? I will not be keeping you from something?"

"Aside from a pile of laundry?" She shook her head. "Besides, I could use a trip into town. I haven't been grocery shopping in over a week." She pointed to a lengthy shopping list taped to the refrigerator door.

Naomi thought a moment longer, then nodded. "Ja, that would be very helpful. *Danki*, Cheryl. I will go and put the things in your car."

"Do you need help?" Cheryl draped the damp dish towel over the edge of the sink then crossed to the door and bent to slip into a pair of shoes.

"*Ne*, I can get it." Naomi motioned toward Rebecca. "You have your hands full anyway." She bent to press one last kiss to the top of Rebecca's head. "Goodbye, my little *schisselblumme*. I will see you tomorrow."

Rebecca watched her go, her eyes as wide as the primrose Naomi had taken to calling her from time to time. When the door closed her from sight, she let out a wail and stretched out her arms to Cheryl for comfort.

"There, there," Cheryl soothed. "Oma will be back." She ducked her head to look in Rebecca's eyes. "Do you want to go see Auntie Esther?"

Rebecca's cries faded as she blinked away the watery crocodile tears.

"I thought so," Cheryl said, laughing as she carried the baby to the bathroom and turned on the tap in the tub. "But first, let's get those cookie crumbs out of your hair."

Lots of suds and giggles later, Cheryl pulled up to the Swiss Miss, a sleeping Rebecca snoring softly in her car seat, her flushed cheeks and rosy lips making her look angelic in the rearview mirror. Smiling, Cheryl climbed from the car and then tucked the sleeping baby into a stroller before making her way inside.

As always, the sounds and smells of the store embraced her like an old sweater. As she made her way to the counter, she breathed in the scents of yeasty baked goods, spicy homemade candles, and pungent cheeses. It was a strange mixture but better than any perfume, and it reminded her of Aunt Mitzi. She'd been missing her a lot since she'd gone back to Papua New Guinea.

Esther looked up as Cheryl approached. She bid a hasty goodbye to the young English man she'd been talking to and turned, her cheeks slightly flushed and a lock of her brown hair poking out from beneath her prayer *kapp*. "Hey, Cheryl. I wasn't expecting you today." She scooped up a pile of receipts scattered across the counter and stuffed them into a drawer. "Everything okay at the farm?"

Cheryl raised her eyebrows. Esther *was* young—just turned twenty on her last birthday—but she took her Amish upbringing very seriously, and her speech was normally very proper. Using the casual language that was so common to most English teenagers was rare for her. It was probably just a side effect of spending more time in the store, now that she was full-time, but it still took Cheryl by surprise.

She shook the thought away and pointed to the basket of goods tucked into the storage bin under the stroller. "Supplies from your mom. She said you were out of jam and a few other things?"

Esther circled the counter, her brown eyes sparkling with excitement. "Yep. The sale on homemade bread last week was a hit. Did she tell you?"

She bent over the stroller, the ribbons of her prayer kapp swaying gently as she stroked Rebecca's cheek with her finger. "Sweet baby."

Cheryl instantly relaxed. There was the girl she knew. Esther had taken her vows and joined the Amish church over a year ago, so seeing her conversing with an Englisher and hearing her adopt their way of speaking was unsettling, but she needn't be concerned. She was still the same sweet, responsible Esther.

Esther looked up from the stroller expectantly. "Cheryl?"

"Oh." She blinked free of her thoughts and nodded. "Yes, she told me. The sale was a really great idea, Esther. You're doing a wonderful job here at the store."

"Thanks." Hesitation filled her gaze as she looked toward the door where the young man she'd been talking to was disappearing. "I mean, danki." She brushed her hands down her apron and returned to the cash register. "Anyway, I'll get those items stocked this afternoon, after the lunch rush is over."

Cheryl glanced down at the still sleeping baby. "Why don't I do it for you?"

Two customers, both carrying blocks of Naomi's famous homemade cheese, approached the counter. Esther checked them out and handed them their change with a pleasant smile. When they were gone, she turned back to Cheryl.

"Are you sure you want to do that? It's no problem to wait." She gave a wave that encompassed the store. "I'm sure I'll have time after the next tour bus comes."

"That's okay. I'd be glad to help," she said, and hung her purse over the handle of the stroller. "I'll just push Rebecca over next to me so she's out of the way."

Giving a smile to a couple of customers approaching the counter, she turned the stroller around and wove past the barrels of dry goods until she reached the shelves along the wall where they kept the jars of jams and jellies. Much of the remaining inventory was in disarray, so Cheryl took a moment to straighten everything and turn all the labels out neatly before stocking the new jars.

Rebecca was still asleep when she finished, so Cheryl moved on to another project. A stack of handmade dish towels and aprons needed folding and arranging into a tidy display. She smiled as she worked, wondering why it seemed so much easier to do laundry here at the store rather than at home.

She reached for another towel, upsetting something that had been tucked underneath. It fell to the floor with a soft thump. Puzzled, Cheryl bent down to retrieve it. It was a small Ziploc bag, the kind she used to store Rebecca's snacks. Inside was something that looked like half a cup of oregano, or maybe a bit of dried parsley, or...

Cheryl's eyes widened in shock. She flung the Ziploc down, stepping away from it as though it were a living thing, then crossed her arms and looked hastily around the store to see if anyone watched. It wasn't herbs inside that bag. Unless she was badly mistaken...

It was marijuana.

CHAPTER TWO

Rebecca stirred in the stroller and Cheryl thought she would wake, but then she popped her thumb in her mouth and settled back to sleep. Blowing out a breath, Cheryl pushed the stroller with one hand and picked up the Ziploc with its suspicious-looking contents with the other. Carrying it gingerly by the corner, she hurried to her old office behind the counter. Inside, she stood looking around. She couldn't throw the bag away. It was evidence. She slid open one of the desk drawers, dropped the bag inside, and then turned to lean against the chair.

Marijuana. It had to be. Not that she was an expert, by any means. Still, she'd seen pictures. She wasn't totally naive.

Anger filled her at the thought that someone had dared to bring an illegal substance into the store—her store—where children and families came to shop.

Crossing to the door, she fought to tamp her anger as she searched the store for Esther. Spotting her next to the dairy cooler, she beckoned her over.

"Esther, could you come in here for a moment, please?"

Esther's head lifted, and she nodded. "Sure. Be right there." A moment later, she popped into the office, a cheerful smile on her face. "What's up?"

Cheryl drummed her fingers restlessly against the top of the desk. "Esther, have you seen any suspicious-looking people in the store lately? Anyone who seemed out of place?"

Esther gave a casual shrug. "A lot of people come into the store, Cheryl. What do you mean by suspicious?"

Cheryl slid open the desk drawer and pulled out the plastic bag. "What I mean is, have you seen anyone who might have brought this—?"

"Marijuana?" Esther stepped back from the desk, her eyes widened like saucers. "It's not mine."

"Of course it's not yours. That thought never occurred to me." Cheryl stared at her incredulously. "How do you even know what it is?"

"I..." Her shoes scuffed the floor as she shuffled her feet. "I've seen pictures."

"Really? Where?"

"Um..." Esther put her finger to her lip and began nervously biting her nail.

"Anyway, I suppose that doesn't matter," Cheryl said finally. "What does matter is how it got here in the first place."

Too animated to sit still any longer, she circled the desk and began pacing the floor. "It had to have been left today, so we'll need to go over everyone who's been in since you opened this morning."

"What makes you think it was left today?"

Cheryl stopped pacing to look at her, but Esther turned her face away, refusing to meet her gaze. What on earth was wrong with her? Why was she acting so strangely?

Cheryl squared to look at her. "You did sweep and clean the store yesterday when you closed, right, Esther? And you straightened up and restocked the shelves this morning before you opened?"

Esther grabbed one of the strings of her prayer kapp and began twisting it around her finger. "Of course."

"So then, the bag had to have been left after you cleaned. Otherwise, you would have seen it."

She dropped her gaze and nodded. "Oh. Yeah, I guess so."

Cheryl crossed her arms with a frown. "Well? Can you remember who came in? Anyone who might have stuck out to you?"

Esther lifted one shoulder in a shrug. "I don't know, Cheryl. I didn't really pay that much attention. It was a lot of regulars mostly."

"Mostly?"

"Well, there were a few people I didn't recognize," she said finally, and with a note of defensiveness Cheryl found startling. Esther slipped her hands into the pockets of her apron, her lips pressed together mutinously.

Unease stirred in Cheryl's stomach. Something was definitely wrong. What wasn't Esther telling her? She crossed to the desk and reached for the phone.

Esther jerked as though stung. "Who are you calling?"

"Chief Twitchell." Cheryl gestured to the bag. "We can't leave that here. I have to turn it over to him."

Esther bit her lip hesitantly. "Before you do that…"

"Yes?" Cheryl eyed her curiously.

She motioned to the bag. "A discovery like that could be bad for business. Maybe we should just, I don't know, throw it away or something?"

Cheryl put down the phone and stared at her in disbelief. "No, Esther, we can't just throw it away. It's an illegal substance. We need to report it."

"But..." She glanced over her shoulder at the door and then back at Cheryl. "I thought marijuana wasn't considered dangerous anymore. I thought people were using it for medicine and things like that. Some states are even legalizing it."

Obviously, she'd been talking to someone. Cheryl crossed her arms, fighting to keep her tone even. "Where did you hear that?"

"A f-friend told me," she stammered. After a moment, she lifted her chin and drew her shoulders back. "Is that not right?"

"It's right in some places, Esther, but here, in Ohio, it is still very much illegal." She reached for the phone again and dialed the number to the station. Delores Delgado answered on the second ring. Cheryl gave her a brief explanation of why she was calling and then hung up and returned her attention to Esther. "The police are sending someone down."

Esther gave a curt nod, one that said she was not happy about the situation, and turned for the door. "I will be out here, waiting on customers."

"Esther, wait. I'm sure the police are going to want to speak to you about who you may—"

"Sorry, Cheryl." Esther shook her head firmly. "It's like I told you before, I didn't see anyone or anything suspicious." She glanced at her watch and then motioned toward the store. "It's just about time for the tour bus to arrive. I better get back out there."

Confusion rippled through Cheryl's stomach. Esther should have been surprised by what Cheryl had found. She should have been more upset or worried. Instead, she seemed to be none of those things. In fact, the way she turned on her heel and hurried out of the office almost made it seem like...

Cheryl sank into the chair behind the desk, the sick feeling growing in the pit of her stomach. It had never occurred to her that the drugs might be Esther's. She still refused to believe it. But why had she instantly been so defensive? She had to know more than she was telling.

Rebecca's cry jerked her from her thoughts. Crossing to the stroller, she lifted the baby out and pressed her to her shoulder.

"There, there, Boo. It's all right. Everything's all right."

Except that deep down, Cheryl knew it wasn't all right. And she had no idea how to make it so.

Chapter Three

By the time Cheryl fed Rebecca and changed her diaper, most of the anger and surprise she'd felt when she'd found the marijuana had faded. Officer Ortega had wasted no time coming down from the station, and Cheryl was only too happy to be relieved of the bag, if not her concern.

Finished washing Rebecca's face and hands, she tucked the baby back into the stroller and then ducked out of the office to let Esther know she was leaving. She found her by the coolers, arranging shelves and removing out-of-date items to be replaced with fresh. Spying Cheryl, she straightened and wiped her hands down the length of her apron.

"You are finished with Officer Ortega?"

Cheryl nodded. Rebecca was clamoring for attention, so she took a couple of toys from her diaper bag and gave them to her. "Did she speak to you?"

Esther nodded and shut the door to the cooler carefully. "She asked me the same questions you did. I told her I did not know who the drugs belonged to."

Cheryl frowned sadly. Esther had never lied to her. Before today, she wouldn't have believed her capable. It broke her heart to think Esther's word could not be trusted, but she had to know for certain.

"Was that the truth, Esther?" she asked, softly, meeting her gaze without flinching even when she saw the hurt flicker in Esther's eyes.

"I did not see who left the drugs," she said after a long moment. She lifted her chin and folded her arms across her chest. "That is the truth."

Unfortunately, it didn't answer Cheryl's question. Before she could say so, Esther turned her back and reached for another round of cheese. Cheryl sucked in a breath. Esther was deliberately cutting the conversation short, and that fact settled like a stone in Cheryl's stomach. This whole day felt surreal, like something from a bad dream, and mostly what she wanted was just for it to end.

She reached out and touched Esther's elbow. "I'm sorry. I didn't mean for it to sound as though I was accusing you of anything. I'm just trying to figure out how that stuff ended up in the store."

Esther grew still, but she didn't look at her. She set down the cheese, and her head jerked in a stiff nod. "I understand. It is all right."

"Thank you," Cheryl said, uncertainly.

"What…" Esther turned, the hem of her apron clutched tightly in her hands. "What did Officer Ortega say about the drugs?"

Cheryl cast a quick glance around the store, then took a step toward Esther and lowered her voice. "She said not to worry too much since it was a fairly small amount. Apparently marijuana use is becoming more and more common among high school students. She said one of them probably dropped it."

Relief wiped the lines of worry from Esther's brow. She let go of her apron and propped her hands on her hips. "Oh. Ja, that is probably what happened. So then, it is no big deal."

"I wouldn't say *that* exactly. It's still a big deal." Cheryl reached for the handle on the stroller and gave it a gentle push. "I don't like the idea of someone bringing drugs into the store, and I would appreciate it if you could maybe keep an eye out. I'll ask Lydia to do the same when she's working."

"Of course," Esther said quickly, then dropped her gaze to her shoes and cleared her throat awkwardly. "I am very sorry this happened, Cheryl. I will try to keep better watch over things when I am here."

Affection for her sister-in-law swept over her. Of course Esther wasn't hiding anything. She was just embarrassed that it had happened while she was tending the store and probably thought Cheryl would see it as her fault. She stopped rocking the stroller long enough to wrap her in a hug.

"Thank you, Esther. I know you'll do your best to keep an eye on things. You're doing a great job with the store." She stepped back and held Esther at arm's length. "I hope you don't think I blame you for what happened?"

Flustered by the sudden tears that filled Esther's eyes, Cheryl took a tissue from a pocket in Rebecca's diaper bag and pressed it into her hands.

"Oh, sweetie, please don't worry. It's like Officer Ortega said. It was probably just some kid." She bit her lip nervously. "But I really would like for you to keep an eye out, okay? Maybe we can keep this from happening again."

Esther wiped the dampness from her cheeks with the tissue then shoved it into a pocket of her apron and managed a weak smile. "Okay. I will try."

"Thank you—" Cheryl began.

"Esther? Is everything all right?" Henry Detweiler, the young man who worked across the street in Hoffman's Furniture, circled a row of tables, his long legs carrying him quickly toward them. He gave a nod to Cheryl then dipped his head to peer into Esther's face, concern making his brown eyes appear almost black. "I saw a police officer leaving the store. What happened?"

A blush colored Esther's cheeks as she cut a glance at Cheryl. "Everything is fine, Henry. You need not have concerned yourself."

Henry was a young man, only a year older than Esther, but something about the firm tilt of his chin and the set of his shoulders made him seem much older. "Are you sure? I overheard a couple of women talking outside. They said something about drugs in the store. Is this true? Did someone find drugs here?"

Esther set her mouth obstinately. "The rumors have started already? Does no one in this town have anything better to do?"

"Uh, hello, Henry," Cheryl interrupted, stepping forward to shake his hand. "Thank you for coming."

He gave a quick nod. "Of course."

"Unfortunately, it is true, I did find a small bag of marijuana," Cheryl continued, "but I've already turned it over to the police. That's what Officer Ortega was doing here."

If there was one thing Cheryl had learned from living in a small town, it was that there was no sense in trying to hide the truth. Word always got out. Maybe this way, she could stem some of the gossip.

"Do you know who it belonged to?" Henry's question was directed to Cheryl, but his gaze slid to Esther.

"Not yet," Cheryl said. "Esther didn't remember seeing anyone unusual come into the store, but since Officer Ortega thought it might have belonged to a student, she is going to try and keep an eye out."

Bored with her toys, Rebecca let out a whine and clambered up to her knees inside the stroller. Cheryl scooped her up and bounced her on her hip.

"A student, like from the high school?" Henry's mouth firmed, and his chest rose and fell with his deep breath. "There was a student in the store this morning, an *Englischer* by the name of Zachary Waller. I saw him come in when I was sweeping off the sidewalk."

"Lots of students come into the Swiss Miss, Henry," Esther said, stepping forward quickly.

"Ja, this is true, but Zachary is well known for causing trouble," he replied, setting his hands on his hips. "And it was not just today. He has been coming around a lot."

"So have you. Every day." She crossed her arms and glanced pointedly at the clock on the wall. "Speaking of which, isn't it almost time for your lunch break to be over?"

"Esther," Cheryl chided, surprised by the argumentative note in her voice. "Henry is just trying to be helpful."

Esther cut Henry a look filled with irritation. "Helpful? I don't think so." She stepped toward him, tipping her head back to stare him in the eyes. "Let me remind you that jealousy is a sin, Henry Detweiler, and I'll thank you to keep your opinions about Zach to yourself."

She spun, her apron strings fluttering, and marched away, leaving a stunned Cheryl staring after her.

"What in the world was that all about?"

At his silence, she turned to Henry, but he refused to meet her gaze. Large veins protruded from his neck, and his breathing had quickened. Even his ears were red.

"Henry?" Cheryl said cautiously. "Are you all right?"

He looked at her, his eyes darkened by hurt. "I am fine. I'm sorry, Mrs. Cheryl, but Esther is right. I should be going. Mr. Hoffman will be wondering where I am."

Despite his words, he didn't look fine as he marched toward the door. He gave Esther a wide berth, his shoulders hunched and his gaze fixed to the floor in front of his shoes. Watching him go, Cheryl sighed. Poor Henry. He was a likable young man, and his feelings for Esther were painfully obvious, but...what had she meant when she said he was jealous? Of who? She had to have meant the Englisher, Zachary Waller, but did that mean Esther had feelings for him?

Cheryl hoped not, if what Henry had said about him being a troublemaker was true. Then again, maybe it wasn't fair to base her opinion of Zachary solely on one person's opinion.

She pondered the problem as she settled Rebecca back in the stroller and headed outside toward her car. By the time she turned for home she was clear on one thing—she needed to learn everything she could about Zachary before she spoke to Esther again.

Thankfully, she knew just how she would do it.

CHAPTER FOUR

A warm summer breeze ruffled the hem of Cheryl's skirt as she climbed the steps of the Friendship Mennonite Church. Little Rebecca cooed happily on her hip, her chubby fingers twined in Cheryl's hair.

So much for my hairdo.

Cheryl ran her hand through her tangled curls with a disgusted sigh. Between her unruly locks and Rebecca's, she'd spent nearly thirty minutes in front of the mirror trying to tame their hair into some semblance of order. One step outside and her efforts had been blown to ragged wisps.

Ahead of her, two girls in prayer kapps giggled as they scooted upstairs to the youth room. Such a sight was typical in their church. Many of the members dressed in plain clothes, while others chose to exercise their freedom to dress in English clothes. Their church had a mixture of both.

At least the girls in plain clothes didn't have to worry about unmanageable curls. Their conservative kapps kept their hair neatly hidden from view. Not that tangles were the reason for the kapps but still, days like today made Cheryl question her choice to reject plain clothes when she and Levi married.

The doors opened again, and Levi stepped through. The parking lot was packed with both cars and buggies, and it had taken him a while to find a parking space. His eyes lit as he caught sight of her and the baby, and he quickly took off his hat and wound toward them.

"There you are," Cheryl said, smiling as he bent to press a kiss to her cheek. "I was just about to take Rebecca to the nursery."

Levi held his hands out and grinned at Rebecca playfully. "Let me do it. She doesn't cry as much when I take her."

Rebecca gave a squeal and leaned into Levi's arms. Letting go, Cheryl lifted her hand to her hair. "Well, I could use a minute to freshen up. I'll meet you in the sanctuary?"

He nodded, and Cheryl watched him go, their daughter cradled easily in his arms. At the end of the hall, he looked back at her and winked. Cheryl felt a blush heat her cheeks. Even after a year and a half of marriage, her heart still thumped every time he looked at her with that playful twinkle in his eyes. She hoped it always would.

"Good morning, Cheryl."

Hearing Grace Ladd's familiar voice, Cheryl turned to look for her. Grace looked exceptionally pretty in her pale blue cotton maternity dress.

Cheryl stepped forward to meet her. "Good morning." She dropped her gaze to Grace's belly. "How are you feeling?"

"Tired, and more than a little ready to be done with swollen feet and a sore back." She rubbed her hand over her stomach with a smile. "It'll all be worth it though, when this little one makes his appearance."

Cheryl smiled. "Just keep reminding yourself that you only have a few weeks left to go. And speaking of which, are you excited about your baby shower? It's in two weeks, you know."

Grace nodded eagerly. "The pictures you sent of the invitations and the cake are just darling. Who thought of the 'You knit me together in my mother's womb' theme?"

Cheryl laughed. "I have to admit, I can't take credit. It was my mom's idea. I told her we were going to have a baby shower, and she suggested it. I'm thinking you should be prepared for scads of homemade afghans and little sweaters and onsies."

"No one can knit and crochet like our ladies, that's for sure," said Grace. "Thank you all so much for hosting it for me."

"We're glad to do it." She gave Grace's arm a pat. "Have you and James settled on a name yet?"

"Not yet. James wants to name him after his grandfather but..." She grimaced and rubbed her hand over her belly.

"But?"

"It's hard to find a middle name that goes with Rutherford."

"Oh no." Cheryl couldn't help the laugh that escaped. Grace quickly joined her.

"I'm trying to talk him into shortening it to just 'Ford.' Not sure he's sold on the idea, at least, not yet. But I'm not done trying." She gave an exaggerated wink as James approached with Pastor Lory in tow.

"Hmm." James scratched his head and shot a sidelong glance at Grace. "Why do I get the feeling you two ladies were talking about me?"

"I have no idea, dear," she said, slipping her arm through his. "Morning, Pastor."

"Morning, Grace. Morning, Cheryl."

Pastor Lory was an older man, well into his fifties, with a friendly face and a kind smile for everyone he met. Cheryl gave him a bright smile. "Good morning."

Grace tipped her head back to smile coyly at her husband. "Cheryl and I were just discussing baby names."

"Ah." James rocked back on his heels and hooked his thumbs in his pockets. "So she told you about the family curse."

Cheryl nodded then pressed her hand to her mouth to keep from giggling. "Sorry, James. I'm with Grace on this one."

"Me too," Pastor Lory said behind a hearty chuckle. "I don't know of too many Rutherfords walking around nowadays."

"I know." James groaned and slapped his hand to his forehead. "I suppose I'll have to give in eventually and let her name him Ford."

"I'm glad we're in agreement," Grace said, poking him in the ribs teasingly. "C'mon, James. Let's go get a seat." She turned to Cheryl. "You coming?"

"Actually, Cheryl, I'd like to talk to you a minute if you have time," Pastor Lory cut in.

Cheryl nodded, and Grace pointed toward the sanctuary. "We'll save you guys a seat."

"Thanks." Cheryl gave her a wave and then turned to Pastor Lory. "What's going on, Pastor? Is everything okay at the parsonage?"

Levi and a few other members had recently completed some repair work to the parsonage kitchen, so Cheryl hoped Pastor Lory hadn't come to talk to her about a problem there.

He shook his head briskly. "Oh, no, no. It's not the parsonage. Everything there is fine. Better than fine. Sonya and I are very happy with the new cabinets and countertops. Sonya even said she liked it better than her old kitchen."

"Levi will be so glad to hear that. And here he comes." Cheryl beckoned to her husband. Levi joined them, and she motioned to Pastor Lory. "We were just talking about the new kitchen in the parsonage."

Levi's eyebrows rose. "Everything is okay, I hope?"

"More than okay. Like I told Cheryl here, Sonya is in love." He put out his hand to clap Levi on the shoulder. "Thanks again for heading up that project. I know it was a big job, especially with the repairs to the floor. You really are a master craftsman, Levi."

Levi shrugged, as humble as ever. "There were many hands, not just mine."

"Yes, but taking time out of your schedule probably put you behind on work around the farm. And what about the *dawdy haus* you and Cheryl told me about. How is it coming?"

"Oh, it's all finished, except for some of the furnishings," Cheryl said, excitement creeping into her tone.

Dawdy hauses were traditionally something the Amish built behind their main house for parents and grandparents. It made helping care for them as they progressed in years easier. But Cheryl and Levi intended to make use of their dawdy haus regularly by taking in strangers and missionaries, basically anyone who found themselves in need of a temporary place to stay. She was excited to take on their first visitor.

"I'm glad to hear that," Pastor Lory said. "I may have a family you might be interested in. Would you mind sticking around after the service so we can talk?"

Cheryl and Levi had informed him of their plans for the dawdy haus, and had asked him to keep them in mind if he heard of any families in need, so his request was not surprising.

"Of course," Levi said, shooting a glance at Cheryl, who nodded. "No problem. Thanks for thinking of us, Pastor."

"Great. Thanks, guys. We'll talk later." Pastor Lory glanced at his watch then motioned toward the sanctuary. "We'd better get inside. It's almost time for the service to start."

All through the music service, Cheryl wondered about the family Pastor Lory had spoken about. Who were they? What was their situation?

Once the preaching started, however, she forced herself to concentrate, and was glad she did when the message turned toward resisting the temptations of the world. Pastor's advice of looking to God for strength and using His word to answer the whispered lies of the enemy filled her with confidence. She knew just what she'd say when she talked to Esther again.

After church, while Levi went to the nursery to fetch Rebecca, Cheryl circled back toward the Sunday school rooms to search out a couple of the students. Many of them had attended the youth retreat she'd helped lead last winter, so she felt confident asking them what they knew about Zachary. Spying two of the older teens, Bethany and Kelly, Cheryl motioned them over.

"Mrs. Cheryl!" Always exuberant, Bethany dashed over to her and wrapped her in a tight hug.

"Hey, Bethany," Cheryl said, squeezing back. "How's cheer camp going?"

Bethany's face split in a wide grin. "Great. I made captain."

"Congratulations! That's wonderful." Cheryl gave her an extra happy hug and then turned to Kelly. "How about you, Kelly? Enjoying your summer?"

"I was." She grimaced and flipped a lock of her long brown hair over her shoulder. "Summer league volleyball starts next week."

"You don't want to play?"

"I do, but getting the time off from work is a pain."

"Ah, I see," Cheryl said. "You still working at Dollar General?"

Kelly nodded. Of the two girls, she was much more studious and reserved. Cheryl had always marveled at her friendship with Bethany since outwardly, they seemed to have so little in common. Inwardly, however, they were both very devoted to the church and strong in their faith.

"Well, hopefully you won't have any trouble doing both," she said. She stepped closer. "Listen, do either of you know a boy from school named Zachary Waller?"

The girls exchanged a long glance, and then Kelly nodded.

"Yeah, we know him. He's pretty popular."

Cheryl's thoughts flashed to her high school days, when the way a person looked often earned them the label "popular." But there were other ways into the "in" crowd, some less innocent than others. She shifted her weight to one foot and crossed her arms. "How do you mean 'popular'?"

"Oh, you know." Bethany gave a wave. "He plays football and stuff, so people like him."

"So he's an athlete."

"Yeah. He's pretty good too," Kelly said. "The team made it to the playoffs last year because of him. The problem is, he's always bragging about how he's got scouts coming to watch him play."

"Yeah, but that part's true," Bethany said, patting Kelly's arm. "I saw the ones from Ohio State. They really did come to watch him play."

Kelly shrugged, as though it didn't matter to her one way or the other.

"Interesting," Cheryl said. "So, what else can you tell me?"

Kelly glanced at Bethany for help. "Um, I don't know much about him outside of sports. We don't exactly hang in the same circles. Do you?"

Bethany snorted and gave a toss of her head. "Are you kidding? No way."

"You sound pretty certain," Cheryl said. "Exactly what kind of circles does he run in?"

"The bad kind," Kelly said. She reached for Bethany's arm. "I didn't mean to make it sound like you and him . . . you know. I just thought maybe . . . well, football player, cheerleader . . ." She made a balancing motion with her hands. "Kinda the same thing. I just thought maybe you could tell her more about him since you know the same people."

"I gotcha." Bethany shrugged, looked over her shoulder, then looked at Cheryl. "Zach is kind of a partier. Not bad or anything, just..." She bit her lip uncertainly.

"Drinking and stuff," Kelly finished. "No worse than some of the other kids. I mean, there are quite a few in our class who—"

She broke off and shot a guilty look at Bethany. Obviously, she didn't want to be considered a tattletale, so Cheryl changed the subject.

"Anyway, about Zach? Someone told me he's known as something of a troublemaker."

"That's true, I guess. He has been known to get into a little trouble," Kelly said. She poked her thumb over her shoulder at a group of students heading down the stairs from the youth room and back. "The problem is, kids kinda look up to Zach."

"But he's not exactly the best example?" Cheryl said.

Both Kelly and Bethany shook their heads.

"It's not just us saying so," Bethany added, motioning toward the kids disappearing through the doors. "Pretty much anyone you ask will tell you the same thing, but only a few will say there's anything wrong with it, and that includes some of the teachers and coaches."

Her bluntness shocked the words from Cheryl's mind before she could speak them.

At the look on her face, Bethany giggled and elbowed Kelly in the ribs.

"What she means is, some of the coaches think as long as you don't get caught with anything in school, they really don't care what you do out of school."

"That's it." Bethany pointed in the direction of the parking lot. "Anyway, I've got to get going. My folks are waiting in the car."

Kelly's head bobbed. "Mine too."

Finding her voice, Cheryl nodded. "Oh, right. Thanks for your help, Bethany. You too, Kelly."

"You're welcome."

"Bye, Mrs. Cheryl."

They took off with a wave, leaving Cheryl plenty to think about. Levi and Rebecca were at the opposite end of the hall, so she pasted on a smile and made her way toward them.

Crouching, she took hold of Rebecca's hands and pressed a loud kiss to her silky cheek. "Hello, Boo. How was children's church? Did you have fun?"

Rebecca chatted away, telling her all about her morning in baby talk, with a few actual words scattered in, her favorite one, *cookie*, included.

"You looked like you were having a pretty serious conversation back there." Levi inclined his head down the hall. "Everything okay?"

"Um…" Cheryl picked up Rebecca and took her time straightening her dress and smoothing her curls. "Oh, you know, typical teenage stuff. Have you seen Pastor Lory?"

Levi motioned toward the sanctuary. "He's just finishing up talking with a couple visiting from Charm."

"Oh?"

Cheryl peeked inside the sanctuary. The couple chatting with Pastor Lory was younger than she and Levi, and they had no kids with them. Newlyweds? He was tall and handsome, she, shy and blushing as she stared adoringly at her husband. They looked eager as they shook hands with the pastor and then headed for the exits.

"Maybe some new members?" she said hopefully.

"Maybe." Levi took Rebecca from Cheryl and tipped his head toward the door. "Let's go see what Pastor Lory wants to talk to us about."

The pastor looked up as they approached and tucked a pen into his shirt pocket. "Levi, Cheryl, thanks so much for waiting."

"No problem," Cheryl said.

Pastor Lory held up one of the visitor cards the church kept stocked in every pew. "I was just talking to Roy and Melinda VanderZanden. Did you get a chance to meet them?"

Levi shook his head. "Was that the couple that just left?"

Pastor Lory nodded. "They're newlyweds, looking for a home church."

"They've found a great one," Cheryl said, smiling that she'd been right about the dreamy look on Melinda's face. "Do you think they'll be back?"

"I hope so. They seemed genuinely interested in learning more." Pastor Lory flapped the visitor's card and then slid it into his Bible. "Anyway, maybe you can be on the lookout for them if they do come back? I'd love for them to meet the two of you."

"Of course," Cheryl said, and Levi nodded.

"We will be happy to."

"Great. Thanks, guys. Anyway, that wasn't what I wanted to talk to you about." He motioned toward Rebecca. "Want to come to my office? I've got some toys in there to keep the baby occupied."

Levi nodded and soon they were ensconced in the pastor's office with Rebecca playing happily on the floor.

Levi gave Cheryl's hand a pat and then crossed one long leg over the other. "So, Pastor, what is all this about?"

"Well, I'm glad you asked, Levi. I had a family contact me recently, looking for a place to live." He reached into his desk and took out a small slip of paper with two names and a phone number printed on the front. "Kyle and Wilma Dorman. They have a seventeen-year-old son named Blake. They're moving back to this area and called me asking about a place to rent."

Levi's brows rose. "Moving back?"

"Uh-huh. Wilma's family used to be members here. They moved away when she was ten."

"Did they tell you where they're moving from?" Cheryl asked.

"A little town about sixty or seventy miles north of here called Wellington. Have you heard of it?"

Levi nodded. "My *daed* and I went through there once several years ago. One of his cousins needed help with a barn raising."

"Ah, I see." Pastor Lory nodded. Barn raisings were familiar to everyone in this part of Ohio.

"Well, apparently," he continued, twisting a pencil through his fingers, "Mr. Dorman and his family lived there for several years up until this past February, when he lost his job. He's been steadily making his way south, looking for work."

"What kind of work does he do?" Levi asked.

"Pretty much anything. He was a mechanic at an auto repair shop for almost five years, but he got laid off. He said he's done all kinds of things before and since."

"And he hasn't been able to find a job?" Cheryl picked up a toy train that Rebecca dropped and handed it back to her.

Pastor Lory spread his hands on the desktop. "According to Kyle, no one has been willing to take on a mechanic, at least not for what he was making before he lost his job. He's been working odd jobs here and there, even started taking on harvesting work just to keep the family afloat, but that means moving from farm to farm."

"And his son is a senior." Cheryl shook her head sadly, remembering the times her family moved because of her father's job as a pastor. It was never easy, but it certainly became tougher as she and her brother grew older and made friends they were reluctant to leave.

Pastor Lory sighed. "With Blake entering his last year of high school, his father wants to settle down someplace where they can let him finish out his football career. I thought of you two and the Miller farm."

"Ja, we can certainly find some kind of work to keep him busy, but it will probably not pay what he was used to at the automotive shop," Levi said.

"But if we let them stay in the dawdy haus, maybe they wouldn't need to earn as much," Cheryl said.

Bored with her toys, Rebecca crawled over to Cheryl and whined to be picked up. Cheryl lifted her onto her lap then took a snack cup filled with cereal from her diaper bag. Rebecca grabbed it eagerly and began pulling cereal out of the cup and popping it noisily into her mouth.

"I confess, that is kind of what I was hoping you would say." Pastor Lory pushed the paper with the Dormans' name and phone number on it toward them. "That number is for the hotel where the Dormans are staying. Why don't you take this with you? Pray about it overnight. If it's something you think you can help with, give me a call in the morning."

Levi took the paper, studied the names written on it for a long moment, then slid it into his pocket and stood. "We will do that. Thank you for thinking of us, Pastor Lory. We will call you tomorrow, after Cheryl and I have had a chance to talk."

"That will be fine. Thank you, Levi."

The two shook hands, and then Pastor Lory turned to give Cheryl a hug and Rebecca a tickle under her chin. "Goodbye now. You all enjoy the rest of your day."

Cheryl smiled as she bid him goodbye, but deep down, a large knot had begun forming in the pit of her stomach, thinking of a young boy forced to leave his friends behind right before his final year of high school.

Levi eyed her as they reached the car. He took Rebecca from her and buckled her into her car seat then caught Cheryl's door before she could climb in. Wrapping his arms around her, he pulled her close and pressed a kiss to her head.

"I know that look."

Cheryl pulled back to peer into her husband's face. "What look?"

"The one you are trying, and failing, to hide." He loosened his hold and ducked his head to look her squarely in the eyes. "Are you all right?"

Her dear husband—always so quick to sense her moods and respond to them. Cheryl pressed her hand to Levi's cheek, her fingers tangling in the beard he had begun to grow the day they married.

"I'm all right," she said softly. "But we have a lot to talk about."

Levi's eyes twinkled with mischief. He reached behind her for the door handle and gave it a pull, then swept out his hand to usher her in.

"That, my dear wife, is exactly what I thought you would say."

CHAPTER FIVE

The Miller house on quiet Sunday afternoons was just about Cheryl's favorite place in the whole world. Cheerful voices ringing with love and laughter echoed through every room as preparations began in earnest for the evening meal. Of course, most of the work had been completed the day before, so that all Naomi had to do was put the roast on to cook. After all, Sunday was a day of rest for her too.

A smile brightened her face as Cheryl ducked back into the kitchen. "Rebecca is down for her nap?"

"Finally." Cheryl rubbed her hand over her eyes. "She was really wound up." She crossed to the sink and turned on the tap to wash her hands. "What can I help you with?"

Naomi pointed at a head of lettuce with the tip of the knife she was using to chop onions to add to the roast. "You can put the salad together if you like."

Cheryl sighed happily as she took a large bowl from the cupboard and began tearing pieces of lettuce into it. "Are the men out in the barn?"

Naomi nodded. "Seth wanted to show Levi and Eli the new spreader he bought for next year's planting."

"And the girls?"

"Elizabeth is reading in her room, and Esther went for a walk."

That was good. That meant the family would be occupied long enough for Cheryl to talk privately with Naomi.

"Something on your mind?" Naomi asked, before Cheryl could speak. She pointed to the pile of lettuce accumulating on the counter *next* to the bowl.

"Oh!" Cheryl chuckled wryly as she scooped the lettuce into a colander and rinsed it thoroughly in the sink. "I have been thinking about something that happened at the store. Did Esther tell you?"

"About the drugs?" Naomi nodded. Finished chopping, she pulled the steaming roast from the oven, topped it with the onions, then put it back in to finishing cooking. "I was very sad to hear it. Still no idea where they came from?"

Cheryl shook her head and reached for a tomato to add to the salad. "I thought maybe I would talk to Esther about it again, just to see if she remembered something she'd forgotten before."

Naomi dried her hands on a towel slowly. "Esther told me she did not know where the drugs came from."

"She told me the same thing," Cheryl said. Using the flat side of her knife, she slid the tomatoes into the salad bowl. "I just thought she might have remembered seeing someone come into the store, someone she didn't mention before."

Like Zach. Cheryl debated mentioning his name to Naomi, then decided against it since she knew so little about him. She took two carrots from a bin next to the sink then reached for a peeler.

"Officer Ortega thinks it may have been one of the local kids who dropped it," she said instead.

"A kid?" Naomi's brow furrowed. "Why does she think that?"

"Well, a couple of girls from the youth group at our church told me that drinking and drugs have become quite a problem with kids their age."

Naomi set her spoon down and sighed sadly. "I am sorry to hear that. Young people have many challenges to face these days, for sure and for certain."

Even ones as levelheaded as Esther. Cheryl bit her tongue as she sliced the carrots for the salad. Though she wanted to talk over the situation with Naomi, she owed Esther her respect. After all, it was entirely possible that she was telling the truth about the drugs.

Finished with the salad, Cheryl set the bowl on the table and then went to the sink to wash her hands.

"There, all done." She turned to Naomi. "Anything else you need me to do?"

Naomi shook her head as she sprinkled pieces of fresh parsley over a heaping bowl of homemade macaroni salad. "Everything is done, but the roast will be at least another forty minutes or so, if you'd like to lie down for a bit with Rebecca."

Cheryl thought about it and then hung the towel she'd used to dry her hands over the edge of the counter. "Actually, I think I'm more in the mood for a walk. Would you mind listening for Rebecca in case she wakes before I get back?"

"Not at all." Naomi smiled and shooed her off with a wave of her hand. "Esther was headed down by the pond. If you pass that way, will you send her back here?"

"Sure thing," Cheryl said, already reaching for the knob on the kitchen door.

A pleasant breeze greeted her as she stepped outside, stirring the warm July air just enough to lift the hair from her neck. She smiled as she turned for the pond. She always enjoyed going for walks out here, where the smell of fresh cut hay mingled with corn and animals, even a hint of rain.

She squinted up at the sky, surprised to see that clouds had begun to gather on the horizon. Maybe it was a good idea that she went looking for Esther. She wouldn't want her to get caught in a storm.

Veering slightly, Cheryl made a beeline for the pond. It wasn't far from the house. In fact, when she and Levi were dating, this was one of the places where they used to come to just sit and talk.

As though stirred by her memories, muffled voices drifted through the tall grass and trees clustered along the banks. One sounded like Esther, but the other was deeper and definitely masculine. Who could Esther be talking to, and why out here instead of up near the house?

Cheryl followed the sound of the voices, pushing the grass out of her way until she spied Esther's plain blue dress and stark white prayer kapp. Her back was to Cheryl, but by her sharp movements, she knew Esther was agitated. The young man she was talking to sat perched on a large rock—the same rock where Cheryl had once sat with Levi, discussing their future together.

Cheryl squinted, trying to make out the young man's features. If she wasn't mistaken, it was the same young man that she had seen Esther talking to the day she found the drugs in the store.

Quickening her pace, she stepped from the tall grass. "Esther?"

Hearing her name called, Esther whirled, grabbing for the strings of her prayer kapp. Spying Cheryl, she put her hand to her mouth and said something to the young man then spun back around, a smile that was too wide and too bright to be real pasted to her lips.

"Hi, Cheryl. I didn't hear you coming."

Cheryl's gaze slid to the young man, who was pushing off the rock to slouch next to Esther.

Cheryl gave a nod in his direction. "Who is your friend?"

"This, uh, this is..." Esther's head swiveled toward him and then back to Cheryl.

"Zach Waller," the young man said, stepping forward to extend his hand.

Cheryl gave it a shake, introduced herself, and then turned to Esther. "Your *maam* sent me to find you. Supper is almost ready."

"Of course." She pushed her hands into the pockets of her apron. "I lost track of time. We can go ahead and head back now."

Cheryl didn't budge. Instead, she smiled at Zach and motioned toward the farm. "Zach, would you like to come back to the house to meet Naomi and Seth, Esther's parents?"

Esther sucked in a sharp breath, and Zach quickly shook his head and took a step back.

"No, that's all right. I, uh, just came by to talk to Esther. Thanks anyway." He turned to Esther and gave a nod. "See you later."

"Yeah, okay. See you later, Zach."

Both she and Cheryl watched him go, neither saying a word until the tall grass and trees closed him from sight.

"Esther—"

"You aren't going to tell Maam, are you?" she interrupted, before Cheryl could finish. "Please, Cheryl. Zach stopped by and...we were just talking."

Cheryl crossed her arms. "Esther, this seemed like a lot more than just talking. Why in the world didn't he stop by the house? And why don't you want me to tell your parents?"

Esther threw her hands into the air in frustration. "You know how my parents are. Zach and I are just friends, but Maam and Daed will worry it is something more. They will caution me about 'protecting my heart' and 'keeping myself separate.'"

"Those are very real concerns, Esther. Your parents understand the wisdom of using discernment when it comes to choosing friends."

"But in this case, it isn't about discernment," she insisted, sticking out her chin obstinately. "They will worry simply because Zach is Englisch. You and Maam were friends. How is this any different?"

In the moment that it took for her to frame an answer, Cheryl prayed for wisdom. Finally, she took a step forward and reached out to hug her sister-in-law.

"Esther, you don't really need me to answer that. In fact, I don't think you even want me to. I think you already know what you want and you're just looking for ways to justify it. Am I right?"

Esther's obstinate posture lingered for a long moment, much longer than Cheryl expected. Finally, her shoulders drooped and the stiffness left her spine.

"I guess so. But I really do want my parents to trust my judgment when it comes to my friends. I'm not a child anymore. I wish they would stop treating me like one."

Cheryl let go and stepped back to look into Esther's face. "Look, I won't pretend to know what is going on between you and Zach. Maybe it *is* just friendship, but your parents would be right to worry about it turning into something more, especially if you're not willing to share it with them. As for me, well, I hope you know I will not agree to keep secrets from them. I love them too much to do something like that, not to mention that it wouldn't be right."

"I know," Esther said glumly. She ran her hands over her arms. "But what if they refuse to be fair? What if they don't give Zach a chance?"

"Why would they do that?" Cheryl asked carefully. "Your parents aren't the type to judge others harshly for no reason."

Esther met her gaze steadily. "You already know what Henry told you."

"And?"

She blew out a breath then turned to look out over the pond. "Well, there may be some truth to what he said." She turned back to Cheryl and grabbed hold of her hands, her brown eyes earnest and pleading. "But Zach is different now. I think he really is searching for something." She motioned around her. "That's what we were doing out here. Zach said he had questions. He wanted to talk to me about my faith."

"There's a right way to do things, Esther," Cheryl said doubtfully. "If Zach had questions, he should have come to you openly, not asked to meet with you in private."

"He is embarrassed," she protested quickly, letting go of Cheryl's hands. "He's not ready for people to know that he's searching. That is why he wanted to meet in private." She moved in a circle, flattening the grass beneath her feet with her hurried, anxious steps. "I know Zach has made mistakes, Cheryl. But if we give him a chance, I know he will be someone my parents can accept. He just needs time to figure things out for himself, time my parents will not give him if they think he is an unbeliever."

"But according to what you just told me, he *is* an unbeliever," Cheryl said. "And you have made your vow to the church. You know what that means, Esther."

She stopped pacing and folded her arms over her chest. "Of course I do."

Cheryl raised an eyebrow at the sharpness in Esther's tone.

"Sorry." Esther took a breath and blew it out slowly. "Look, all I want is the same opportunity that you and Levi had. That's not too much to ask for, is it?"

Cheryl drew back, surprised by the tack Esther had chosen. "That's hardly fair, Esther. Levi and I were not looking for a relationship when me met. Besides, we were already both Christians."

"But you were not Amish," she pointed out softly. "Please understand, I do not mean to hurt you with my words. I am glad you and Levi are together. But what would have happened if my parents had refused to accept you simply because your faith was different from theirs?" She waited a long moment and then spread her palms wide. "Zach is in a different place in his faith journey. Is it fair to hold that against him? He *is* searching. That should count for something."

She didn't agree, but Esther had successfully put her in the uncomfortable position of feeling like a hypocrite if she said so. Worse, Cheryl had the sneaking suspicion that was exactly what she had intended.

She frowned and shifted her hands to her hips. "Listen, Esther, I agree that it wouldn't be fair to hold Zach's past against him. Everyone has made mistakes they aren't proud of, but"— she held up her hand before Esther could interrupt—"the Scriptures are very clear about choosing your friends wisely. If Zach really is just a friend, then I think you need to be honest with your parents. Be open with them now, before they hear about your friendship from someone else and assume there is more to your relationship than there is. And if the marijuana we found turns out to be his—"

"It isn't," she insisted firmly.

"Okay, but think about this. Do you really want your parents to hear about Zach's past from someone who might not be friendly to his cause? You, at least, would be able to tell them about him in your own way. You could even explain that he's repented of his mistakes, if indeed he has."

Lines creased Esther's brow while she thought. Finally, she bit her lip and shrugged. "You're right. It would be better coming from me."

A sigh of relief built in Cheryl's chest, but before she could release it, Esther jammed her hands on her hips and continued.

"And I will tell them... after we prove that the marijuana you found wasn't Zach's."

"Wait." Cheryl blinked in surprise. "What?"

"Cheryl, you *have* to help me prove Zach's innocence. Otherwise, nothing else I say will make any difference."

"That wasn't exactly what I had in mind," she began, but Esther forged ahead quickly, her words flying so fast and furious, Cheryl barely had time to think.

"I know the drugs weren't Zach's, but I have no idea how to go about proving it. What good is pleading his case if I don't have any facts to back up my words? And you know everything there is to know about solving mysteries. I know you can figure this one out if you just try." She stuck out her lip, and her voice took on a note of poutiness. "Zach is not at all like what Henry said. I know you'll like him if you give him a chance. Please, Cheryl? Will you help? I'll do whatever you say, whatever I can do to help. You just tell me what to do."

"Okay, okay, slow down now, Esther," she said, when the girl finally paused to draw a breath. "It's not as easy as all that. I have a family now, and a baby who needs me. I can't just drop everything and go running about willy-nilly looking for clues."

"I can help with Rebecca," Esther offered quickly. "Lydia is full-time now, plus I think I could get one of the girls from church to help out if you need someone to watch her."

It was no wonder the store was doing so well under Esther's leadership. She could talk circles around a used car salesman. Cheryl gave in with a laugh and a shake of her head.

"All right, all right. I give. I'll see what I can do."

"Thank you, Cheryl!" Esther's eyes sparkled as she grabbed Cheryl's hands and swung her around, then finished with a giant hug. "Thank you so much."

"You're welcome." She returned Esther's hug then pulled back to cup her cheeks. "But I meant what I said about being open with your parents. It's not right to keep things from them, Esther. Promise me you won't keep sneaking around behind their backs?"

A bit of the exuberance dimmed from her smile, but she nodded and clasped her hands together tightly. "Ja, I'm sure you're right. I promise, I'll try to find the right moment to talk to Maam about Zach."

"Good. That's good," she said. Except...

Esther had given her word that she would speak to her parents. Still, something about the way she cut her gaze away before Cheryl could look into her eyes didn't bode well. That, combined with the color creeping into her cheeks and her rapid breathing made doubt linger in Cheryl's brain. All of those things reminded her of how she felt whenever she was trying to put something past her parents.

And it was usually when she was lying.

CHAPTER SIX

A bullfrog croaked, his low, throaty call rumbling on the moist, summer air. Cheryl sucked in a breath and let it out slow, wishing she could as easily blow away the unease stirring in her belly. Esther had never lied to her before, so why did she still feel so uncomfortable?

"Esther, are you—?"

Esther jabbed her thumb over her shoulder at almost the same instant. "Shouldn't we be going? I thought you said Maam wanted me back at the house."

Cheryl cast a glance up the trail toward the farm. "Yes, that's true. But I really don't feel like we've finished our conversation. Maybe we could talk some more after supper?"

Esther shook her head before she even finished. "I'm sorry, Cheryl. I have a singing tonight. I promised my friends I would be there. Could we do it later?"

Cheryl shuffled her feet in the loamy earth surrounding the pond. Singings were something she'd learned about since moving to Amish country. They were very important to the younger generation, and she wouldn't ask Esther to miss one because of her doubts.

She waved away her concerns and smiled. "That's all right. We'll talk another time."

Esther half-turned to walk back toward the house then stopped and tossed a glance over her shoulder at Cheryl. "Are you coming?"

Cheryl shook her head and pulled her phone from her pocket. "I'll be along. The sun is so pretty over the pond. I just want to snap a few pictures for Rebecca's room. We're still decorating, and I think a few black-and-white shots of the farm would look really nice."

Esther hesitated a moment and then gave a wave and disappeared through the grass. Watching her go, Cheryl sighed. Esther wasn't her daughter, but she did have one. What would she do when Rebecca got to be Esther's age... no longer a child, but lacking the maturity and wisdom to be called an adult? How would she act with her? Of course, she had Levi to help her through the rough spots.

Guilt flooded over her at not having spoken to her husband about her doubts. He was Esther's brother, after all. But besides keeping her friendship with Zach a secret, had Esther really done anything wrong?

After taking several pictures, Cheryl shoved her phone back into her pocket and spent a few minutes in quiet prayer. When she said "amen" her soul felt lighter, like a weight had lifted. She still didn't have a clear answer about what to do with Esther, but she was confident it would come in time.

Voices drifted through the open windows as Cheryl returned to the house. Her husband's voice was among them, deep and strong and cheerful. Her heart warmed just listening. She pushed open the kitchen door and stepped inside.

"Ach, there she is." Naomi pressed a dish into Elizabeth's waiting hands and shooed her toward the dining room. "We were just getting ready to eat."

"How is the pond this afternoon?" Seth leaned against the counter, his hand stroking his beard, one much fuller than Levi's. Of course it would be, since he and Naomi had been married so much longer. He pushed off the counter and directed his gaze through the farmhouse window. "I've been worried about the water level. We could use a goot rain."

"Uh..." Cheryl crossed to the sink and pushed her sleeves to her elbows. "I didn't see too much of a difference," she said, turning on the tap to wash her hands. That was as truthful as she could be since she hadn't actually looked. She'd been too wrapped up in her conversation with Esther to note the water level.

Esther made a small peep, one that drew the glances of everyone in the room. Clearing her throat, she scooped up a bowl of steaming carrots and kept her head lowered as she scooted out of the room with them.

Levi came up behind Cheryl and claimed her waist with his arms. "Everything okay?" he whispered, his warm breath tickling the skin below her ear.

Rebecca's cry spared her from answering. Cheryl dropped the towel she'd been using to dry her hands onto the counter then slipped from Levi's grasp toward the hall. "I'll get her. She probably needs to be changed."

Naomi tilted the pot that she'd cooked the carrots in. It was still partially full and steaming. "I'll mash some of these up for her with a little cold milk."

"Thank you, Naomi."

Cheryl's cheeks warmed as she ducked into the bedroom to care for little Rebecca. She would have to talk to Levi eventually. They did not keep secrets from one another. This was a hard and fast rule. Granted, it was an unspoken rule, but still.

Rebecca's snuggles comforted Cheryl as she walked back into the dining room. The blessing had been said, and the family was already laughing and chatting while they enjoyed their meal. Levi had situated a high chair between his seat and Cheryl's, so she tucked the baby into place before reaching for the platter of roast to add to her plate and Rebecca's bowl of mashed carrots. Across from her, Esther was eating fast. Her plate was almost empty. Cheryl tried not to watch as Esther scooped the last few bites into her mouth and stood.

"May I be excused?"

Seth's lowered brows said he did not approve. Meals were something to be savored in this house, and the family usually stayed gathered around the table talking until everyone had finished. But Naomi touched his hand and bent her head toward his. Finally, Seth nodded.

"All right, Esther. But please stay to help your sister clean the kitchen before you head to the singing."

"Ja, Daed. I will." Esther smiled and picked up her plate, her gaze flashing to Cheryl and then away. "I may be a little later than normal tonight."

Naomi's gaze was curious, but she said nothing.

Seth nodded. "Danki for letting us know. Be sure it is not too late."

"I will." Dishes clattered in Esther's hands as she picked up a couple of empty bowls and added them to her plate. Her plain skirt swishing, she turned and disappeared into the kitchen.

"Esther must be excited about the singing tonight. I have never seen her in such a hurry to leave," Levi quipped, his blue eyes sparkling.

Had Rebecca not been between them, Cheryl would have nudged him to silence with her foot. As it was, she took a hasty swallow from her water glass and ended up choking and reaching for her napkin to cover her cough.

"Cheryl, are you all right?" Reaching out to pat her back, Naomi pressed a second napkin into Cheryl's hand.

"Yes. I'm fine," she managed finally, blinking away the tears that sprang to her eyes. "It just went down the wrong pipe. I'll be fine."

And she would. She only hoped she could say the same for Esther.

CHAPTER SEVEN

Cheryl left Rebecca with Naomi the next day, before heading out do a little last-minute shopping for Grace's baby shower and to secure an extra bed and a new dresser for the dawdy haus. She and Levi had talked it over, and they both wanted to help the family that Pastor Lory had told them about, though Cheryl may have felt more strongly about it than Levi. She just couldn't shake the image of young Blake, forced to move his senior year and leave all of his friends behind.

Sunshine beamed down on Cheryl's head and glinted off the plate glass windows of Hoffman's Furniture store as she stepped from her car onto the sidewalk. She liked Hoffman's. They were known for their fine, hand-crafted merchandise, but more than that, Jacob Hoffman was a friend. Cheryl and Levi had done business with him when they were furnishing their home and, as a thank-you gift, Jacob had crafted a lovely wooden rocking chair when he heard she and Levi were expecting.

She pushed open the door and was immediately greeted by Jacob's booming voice.

"Cheryl! *Guten morgen*, my friend." Pushing out from behind the long counter that ran along the back of the store, Jacob hurried toward her, his hand outstretched. "What brings you by this morning? Time for another rocking chair?"

He tipped his head toward her, his merry blue eyes twinkling.

Cheryl chuckled and shook her head. "Actually, a rocking chair would be nice."

Jacob's face lit, and Cheryl laughed and raised her hand. "Not for me, for Grace Ladd. Her shower is in two weeks. Levi and I thought it would be a nice baby shower gift."

"Aww. That is too bad." He clutched the broad suspenders clipped to his trousers and rocked back onto his heels. "But I am sure Grace will enjoy a rocking chair. And if you and Levi suddenly have a need for another one, you be sure and let me know."

"I'll do that, Jacob," Cheryl said with a laugh.

"So then, what else can I do for you? Anything in particular?"

"Actually, yes." She pointed to her left, where a long line of handcrafted bedframes lined one wall. "Levi and I are about to have guests in the dawdy haus. I need one more bed for the small guest room. It will only fit a twin size."

Jacob's bushy eyebrows rose. "I did not realize the dawdy haus was finished. But you say you are going to have guests? Will it be family? Surely not Seth and Naomi. They are much too young to retire."

"Not family," Cheryl said. "At least, not yet. Levi and I plan to use it as a hospitality house for visiting missionaries or families in need."

"Oh, I see." Jacob gave a quick nod and rubbed his chin thoughtfully. "That is a wonderful idea."

"Thank you, Jacob. The family who will be staying there have a teenage son, which is why I'm looking for something for the other bedroom." She motioned toward the beds. "Mind if I take a look?"

"Not at all." Jacob smiled broadly and waved her that way. "Take your time. If you see something you like, holler. Either Henry or I will be glad to help."

At the mention of Henry, Cheryl craned her neck to look for him. His back was to her as he straightened inventory around the front of the store. She nodded to Jacob and smiled.

"Okay. Thanks again, Jacob. I'll look for you if I have any questions."

He gave her one last smile and bustled off, his large boots scuffling against the hardwood floor.

Focused now on finding what she needed, Cheryl wound slowly around a variety of tables and chairs toward the beds. It always amazed her to see the kind of craftsmanship and detail that Jacob and his men put into the furniture they made. They were artisans, for sure and for certain.

Realizing she'd coined one of the phrases her husband used, Cheryl smiled. It seemed the longer she and Levi were together, the more alike they were becoming, and she didn't mind that one bit.

The first few beds she came to were slatted, with matching head- and footboards. Though they were beautiful, Cheryl passed them up quickly. What she was looking for was something a little more solid, with cleaner lines and possibly some storage underneath.

Farther down the row, she found one that boasted paneled inlays. It also had three built-in drawers that slid under the frame. She reached for the price tag, and was pleased with what she saw. It even had a dresser to match.

"This one is perfect."

She looked around for Jacob, but he was busy helping other customers. Henry, however, stood a few feet away holding a broom. Cheryl crossed to him and tapped him on the shoulder.

"Excuse me, Henry. Would you mind—?"

She cut off as he turned to her. Henry had a black eye, and not just a small bruise. A real shiner.

She jerked in surprise. "Oh my goodness, Henry. What in the world happened to your eye?"

Henry's hand rose to cover the bruise, and he ducked his head self-consciously. "You mean this? It's nothing." He motioned toward the bed Cheryl had been considering. "Did you need help with something?"

She glanced over her shoulder at the bed and back at him. "Oh...well...yes, I'm interested in buying that bed, but..."

She bit her lip and tried hard not to stare at his eye. "I'd like the matching dresser as well. Also, a rocking chair like the one Jacob made for Levi and me when we were expecting Rebecca."

"No problem. I can write it up for you. Will it be a delivery?"

"Yes," she said, following him toward the counter. "Normally, Levi would come by and pick it up himself, but he's been really busy at the farm. Plus, he's still helping his parents with the petting zoo."

Henry's head bobbed. "Ja, I am sure summer is a busy time for the Millers."

He cleared his throat softly as he reached for the ticket and wrote up Cheryl's purchase. "Um . . . if I may ask, how is Esther?"

"Esther?"

He cleared his throat and dropped his gaze to the pencil he was twiddling between his fingers. "Have you seen her this morning?"

"Not yet," she said, "but I'm going over to the store after I leave here. I have a few things I need to pick up."

"Oh. I see."

He sounded so disappointed, it instantly piqued Cheryl's curiosity. But she also felt something else—a suspicion that Henry's black eye and his concern for Esther were related.

Cheryl leaned forward and placed both hands on the counter. "Henry, what happened to your eye?" she asked quietly. "Did something happen at the singing last night?"

He looked up, his brown eyes wide. "Esther told you about the singing?"

It was an odd question, but Cheryl did her best to hide her surprise. She nodded firmly. "She told me she was going. What happened, Henry?"

His jaw hardened, and he looked away. "It is perhaps not for me to say."

"But you're worried about her," Cheryl persisted.

He gave a reluctant nod. "Ja, I am worried." His gaze locked with Cheryl's, and he lifted one brow. "Have you learned any more about the drugs you found at the Swiss Miss?"

"Unfortunately, no. We still have no idea who the drugs belonged to." She studied him curiously.

His fingers tightened around the pencil, turning his knuckles white. "But I *saw* Zachary go into the store that day. They had to be his."

"Lots of people went into the store, Henry," Cheryl said quietly, watching as a flush crept over his cheeks. "You really don't care much for Zach, do you?"

He pressed his lips together and shook his head. "It is not that I do not like him. I just think he could be a lot more trouble for Esther than she realizes."

"Have you told her this?" Cheryl asked.

His shoulders slumped, and he lowered his gaze to the counter. "I have tried. She will not listen."

"Well, you're sweet for trying, Henry, but Esther is a smart girl with a good head on her shoulders. Maybe you should give her a little room to make this decision for herself, even if you don't like the choice she makes. If you don't, you may just end up pushing her away and losing a good friend."

A look of deep hurt flashed across Henry's face, one he quickly hid by bowing his head and shuffling the tickets on the counter. "You are probably right. I just—"

Whatever he'd been about to say, he cut himself short and held up the ticket. "Anyway, here is your order. I will see to it that the bed and dresser get delivered tomorrow."

"That'll be great, Henry. Thank you."

Cheryl gave him her bank card and waited while he rang up her purchases. It was hard not to feel sorry for the guy. His affection for Esther was plain to see, to Cheryl anyway but maybe not Esther. She, apparently, only had eyes for Zach.

Cheryl tried hard to hide her disapproval of Zach as she tucked her receipt into her purse and left the store. Of the two young men, she definitely liked Henry better. He had a gentle way about him that appealed to her, so different from Zach's brash confidence. But then again, it wasn't so much her opinion that mattered. It was Esther's.

And speaking of Esther...

Cheryl crossed the street and made a beeline for the Swiss Miss. Inside, shoppers from a tour bus crammed the aisles, but Zach wasn't among them. Cheryl couldn't help but feel relieved as she packed the items she needed into a basket and crossed to the cash register to check out. Esther did not seem flustered by the number of customers. She greeted Cheryl with a wave and took the basket from her with a smile.

"Good morning, Cheryl. You're in town early." She glanced around her then back. "Rebecca's not with you?"

"Not today. Your mother is watching her."

While Esther checked her out, she explained about the family Pastor Lory had told them about.

"Levi and I both think the dawdy haus would be perfect for them, but we still needed a bed for the guest bedroom." She hitched her thumb toward the door. "I just left Hoffman's. They're going to deliver it tomorrow."

Esther's face went curiously rigid. She picked up a block of cheese and let it fall into the sack with a thump. "You were at Hoffman's?"

Cheryl's suspicions about Henry's black eye solidified. Unfortunately, they wouldn't be able to discuss it here since a line had begun forming behind her. She took her purchases and handed Esther a couple of bills from her wallet.

"I'm curious about what happened last night," she said quietly. "Maybe you can tell me about it later?"

Esther gave a solemn nod, and Cheryl collected her things and left. If she hurried, she'd have time to get home and straighten up a bit before Pastor Lory came by with the Dormans. She and Levi and Pastor Lory had all thought it a good idea that they meet before the family moved in, and Cheryl wanted to make a good impression. She made a quick stop at the Millers' farm to pick up Rebecca before turning toward home.

Levi's truck was already in the driveway. Reminded that she still needed to talk to him about Esther, Cheryl sighed and slung the diaper bag over her shoulder then scooped up Rebecca and headed inside.

One thing at a time, she told herself. For now, all she had to think about was the family she and Levi were going to help. She would worry about everything else later. Much later. Maybe tomorrow.

She grimaced as she reached for the doorknob. *Right. Worry about it tomorrow, Scarlett.*

With that thought in mind, she pasted a smile to her lips, hitched Rebecca higher on her hip, and stepped through the door.

CHAPTER EIGHT

Kyle and Wilma Dorman were nothing like what Cheryl had expected. Wilma was a small woman, very shy, but pretty, in a sweet and understated kind of way. Their son, Blake, looked very much like her except for his height. That, he definitely got from his father—whom he apparently was not very happy with at the moment. He shot several dark glances his way, and when he wasn't glaring, he stared sullenly at the floor. Cheryl chalked it up to teenage angst, a condition compounded by having left his friends behind his senior year.

Along with being tall, Kyle Dorman had a full head of dark, wavy hair and a ready smile. He also had a reckless way about him that made him seem much younger than his wife, though from what they had said, they met in high school, dated through college, and married soon after graduation.

Cheryl filled several glasses with tea and then sat next to Levi on the couch to listen to Kyle explain how he'd hoped to open his own garage, a plan that had been cut short when he lost his job several months back. Fortunately, Rebecca had settled down for her nap just as Pastor Lory and the Dormans arrived, so Cheryl could give them her undivided attention.

Kyle reached for one of the glasses and took a drink. "Anyway, that's how we ended up here," he said, wiping his mouth on a napkin. "It's been a hard road, but one that has definitely brought me and my wife closer together, right sweetheart?"

Reaching out with his free hand, he patted Wilma's knee. Next to them, Blake gave a strangled grunt and rolled his eyes. "Please."

Kyle chuckled and set his glass down on the coffee table. "The boy never has liked it when his mother and I show affection to one another, ain't that right, son?"

"Kyle," Wilma chided quietly. She offered a nervous smile to Cheryl and took one of the glasses of tea for herself. "Thank you."

"You're very welcome." Cheryl picked up another glass and handed it to Pastor Lory.

"Thank you, Cheryl." He too took a drink and then motioned toward Levi. "So, Levi, why don't you tell Kyle a little about the work he would be doing on the farm?"

"Of course." Levi leaned forward to brace his elbows on his knees. "Mostly, it will be caring for livestock, cleaning stalls, helping with the harvesting, and so forth. Do you have any experience with these things, Mr. Dorman?"

He gave a wave and followed it with a soft chuckle. "Please, call me Kyle. I reckon we'll get to know each other pretty well, so we might as well lay off the formalities, right?"

Levi gave a nod. "Very well, Kyle. And please, call me Levi."

"Levi it is." He clapped his hands together, startling Blake, whose gaze bounced from Cheryl to Levi.

"Anyway," Kyle continued, "yes, I do have some experience with farming. I guess the pastor here told you I've sorta been working my way south, picking up odd jobs wherever I could find them, including a couple of farms. Of course, I haven't worked anywhere like the outfit you Millers have here. That corn maze is pretty amazing, and the petting zoo too. But I've done a bit of planting and trimming and such. And my son, Blake,"—he reached around Wilma and hitched his thumb toward the teenager—"he'll be glad to pitch in where he can as well, when he's not playing football, that is."

"Blake is an All-State wide receiver." Wilma draped her arm around her son's shoulders, her eyes shining with pride.

"Really? That's quite an accomplishment," Pastor Lory said. "Congratulations, Blake."

"That was last year," Blake said, his cheeks taking on a ruddy flush.

"I'm sure you'll make it again," his mother said quietly. "Especially now that we're settling down in one place."

Instead of looking pleased, Blake merely grunted and shrugged out from under her arm.

Kyle propped his hands on his knees and smiled broadly at Cheryl and Levi. "Anyway, suffice it to say, we are very grateful for the two of you opening up your home this way."

"It is no trouble. We are glad to do it," Levi said.

Kyle nodded. "Well, we appreciate it. And I have to say, I'm really looking forward to settling down here in Sugarcreek. It seems like a really nice place."

A phone beeped, and Blake rose and pulled one with a distinctive silver apple on the back from his pocket. An iPhone? And the newest version to boot. Hadn't that just come out last—?

"Blake." Wilma gave a slight shake of her head and directed a pointed glance at the spot on the couch he'd vacated. "Not now."

Blake's gaze narrowed angrily. "It's the coach. I have to take it."

"Oh, let him go, Wilma," Kyle said, leaning back against the couch and folding his hands over his stomach indulgently. "Go ahead, Son, but make it quick, eh?"

Blake's chest rose and fell heavily before he turned for the door.

"He's been waiting on that call," Kyle explained once Blake stepped from the room. "Apparently, there are rules about kids who just moved into the school district being eligible to participate on a varsity team. The coach from Blake's last school has to sign off on some kind of form—"

"A previous participation waiver," Wilma said, then lifted her glass to her lips quickly and took a sip.

Kyle snapped his fingers. "Yeah, that's it. The coach here explained it's to keep schools from recruiting players, but we'll all be very disappointed if he's not allowed to play."

"Goodness, I didn't realize it could be a problem," Cheryl said. "Does it look like that might happen?"

"The coach here said it shouldn't be any trouble so long as the coach from his old school will sign off," Wilma said. She lowered her head. "He was...we used to be pretty good friends, so I don't think he'll give Blake any trouble."

"Well, I hope it all works out." Pastor Lory tipped his head toward Kyle. "Please let me know if there is anything I can do to help."

Kyle clapped him on the arm. "I'll do that, Pastor. Thank you."

Levi rubbed his hands together and rose. "So now, would you like to take a tour of the farm, Kyle?"

He jumped to his feet eagerly. "That'd be great. I'll holler at Blake."

Pastor Lory rose with them, and Kyle turned to pump his hand. "Thank you so much for your help. Wilma and I really appreciate you finding this place for us. I don't know where we would have gone otherwise."

"It was my pleasure. And I think you'll find that Cheryl and Levi are excellent hosts."

"I'm sure they are. Everyone has been so friendly here." He shot a grateful smile toward Cheryl and then followed Levi to the door.

"Well, I really should be going," Pastor Lory said, turning to Cheryl.

She gave him a pat on the shoulder and followed him to the door. "We'll see you Wednesday."

"Yep. See you then." He paused at the door and looked at Wilma. "Goodbye, Wilma, and good luck. And if you don't have other plans, we'd love to see you, Kyle, and Blake on Wednesday too. We've got a great program for youth."

She blushed, her hands twisting at her middle. "Thank you, Pastor. I'll speak to Kyle. Goodbye."

Just as Cheryl waved and shut the door behind the pastor, Rebecca let out a loud cry from her nursery.

"Oops. There's the baby. I'll grab her and then I can show you the dawdy haus."

A smile brightened Wilma's face. "That would be wonderful. Thank you. I can't wait to see it."

She bent to pick up the half-empty glasses of iced tea. Cheryl hurried over to stop her.

"Oh, Wilma, you don't have to do that. I'll take care of them when we get back."

She shook her head. "It's no trouble. I'll take care of these while you see to the baby."

That was nice, Cheryl thought as she walked down the hall. Having another woman around might be a blessing.

Rebecca had wet through her clothes, so by the time Cheryl had her cleaned up and changed, Wilma had taken care of all of the dishes and stacked them neatly in the sink. Cheryl joined her in the kitchen.

"Oh my, what a precious little girl," Wilma exclaimed, crossing over to give Rebecca's tummy a tickle. "Look at you, sweet thing."

Rebecca giggled, and Wilma rewarded her with another tickle. "How old is she?"

"Fifteen months," Cheryl said, sitting her on the counter and holding her steady while she filled a sippy cup with water. Handing the cup to Rebecca, she motioned to Wilma. "Eventually, I need to stop referring to her age in months, but it just seems like yesterday that she was born."

Wilma laughed. "It took me a while to stop doing it too, when Blake was a baby."

Cheryl scooped Rebecca off the counter and started for the door. "Ready to see the dawdy haus?"

"Oh, yes. Just let me grab my purse. I left it in the living room." Wilma returned a few seconds later with the purse dangling from her arm. "Okay, I'm ready."

Cheryl led the way outside, with Rebecca tugging happily at her hair.

"So, tell me about this dawdy haus," Wilma said as they descended the back steps and crossed the narrow strip of lawn that separated the main house from the dawdy haus. "It's like a mother-in-law cottage, right?"

"I suppose it would be considered the same thing. Basically, it's a retirement home." Cheryl shifted Rebecca onto her other hip and gestured above them. "Eventually, we'll build a breezeway to connect the two homes, but for now, it works keeping the houses separate."

Wilma lifted her eyebrows. "Why connect them?"

Cheryl pulled a key to the dawdy haus from her pocket and fitted it into the lock. "Well, the Amish don't pay or receive Social Security. They believe it's their children's responsibility to look after the elderly. But they don't sit idle. Usually, the mother helps with the grandchildren and the father continues helping on the farm. A breezeway makes it easier for the family to travel back and forth between the two homes, especially for the older couple when the cold weather hits. It's a great system, really."

"Assuming one likes their in-laws." Wilma gave a wry laugh. "My mother-in-law, for example..."

Cheryl paused to look back at her, and Wilma waved her hand in the air. "Oh, well, never mind. It's all water under the bridge anyway." She grimaced and motioned toward the door. "After you."

"Okay. Come on in." She stepped inside and then moved to make room for Wilma.

Wilma stopped just inside the door, her head swiveling as she took in the large living room, flanked by a hall on one side and a door that led to a half-bathroom on the other. "Wow. This is lovely."

"Well, we wanted it to be comfortable." She pointed to her right. "Bedrooms are that way. There are two. The master is the larger room. There's also a washing machine in the laundry closet down the hall. We have a dryer, but it's broken and the part is on back order. In the meantime, you're welcome to use the clothesline behind the house." She motioned toward the back of the room where an opening larger than a door gave a glimpse of cabinets and a gleaming stainless steel refrigerator. "As you can see, the kitchen is straight through there. Nothing fancy, but I think it should have everything you need."

"Semi-open concept. I like it." Wilma marveled as she walked through the rooms, her voice carrying back to Cheryl with small exclamations of delight here and there. Finally, she returned to the living room, a wide smile on her face.

"What a cute little house. Did you design it yourself?"

"Actually, it's patterned after the main house, with a few touches that I got from my aunt's cottage in town. Like the fireplace." She motioned toward the stone hearth. "Aunt Mitzi always loved a nice fire. I got used to having one on cold winter nights when I was staying in her cottage."

"Well, I for one am sure glad you put it in." Wilma ran her hand over the mantel in approval. "Is this barn timber?"

Cheryl nodded. "It is. Levi's father gave it to us from one of the old family barns that needed to be torn down. A little piece of history."

"Those touches really make a place special."

Rebecca whined to be let down, so Cheryl set her on her feet and watched her scurry off toward the kitchen.

"Well, I suppose I should give you this." She handed Wilma the key and then slid her hands into her pockets. "Let me know if you need another copy made. We have the original up at the main house."

She led Wilma in the direction Rebecca had taken. In the kitchen, she opened the pantry door and showed her the stacks of cans and supplies she had loaded inside. "I stocked a few dry goods for you too, just to get you started. Once the harvest starts, you're welcome to help yourself to anything you need. We grow plenty of vegetables, and Levi and I have added a few fruit trees."

"Oh my goodness...that's so generous." Wilma blinked several times then looked away. As though she weren't quite sure what to do with her hands, she lifted them and let them fall to her sides. "I really don't know what to say."

The sight of her grateful tears warmed Cheryl's heart. She smiled and crossed to rub Wilma's arm. "It's no trouble. We're glad to do it. And I know Levi is going to appreciate the extra help this summer, so it's a win for both of us, really."

"I'm glad you think so," Wilma said. She bit her lip and forced a watery smile. "Anyway, we're hoping to move in Thursday, if that's okay. We're paid up at the hotel where we're staying until the end of the week, but we might be able to get some of our money back if we check out a couple of days early."

"Of course. That will be fine." Cheryl motioned toward the bedrooms. "I'm having some furniture delivered tomorrow for Blake, so after that, you should have everything you need. And feel free to add any personal touches you might like."

"Personal touches?"

She smiled and gestured toward the empty walls. "You know, like photographs and such."

"Oh, right." Wilma gave herself a shake. "Sorry. I wasn't thinking. Yes, I have a few things, but mostly, we just brought what we could carry when we lost the house. Kyle sold everything else trying to keep us afloat."

The smiled slipped as pity welled inside Cheryl's heart. "I'm sorry."

Wilma's jaw tightened and she flipped her hair over her shoulder. "I'm over it. It's just things, right?"

"Uh, right." Spying Rebecca trying to climb onto one of the chairs, Cheryl hurried over to her and swept her up into her arms. "Well, we'd better get back up to the house. This little one is going to need some supper soon."

"Okay." Wilma followed her to the front door and then held it wide while Cheryl passed through. "Listen, if you ever need a babysitter, I'd be glad to help out."

Cheryl shifted Rebecca to her hip while she locked the door. "That's sweet of you, Wilma. Thank you."

She shrugged. "No problem. I used to work in a daycare, so I have references if you need them."

"I'll keep that in mind," Cheryl said with a smile. "So, are you thinking about going back to work? I could ask around for you, see if one of the local daycares is hiring."

"Oh…well…" Wilma's gaze darted around the room. "Actually, Kyle and I thought it might be best for me to stay home for a while, at least until we get settled."

"I understand. That makes perfect sense." She motioned toward the door. "Come on, let's go on back to the house. I'll fix us some coffee while we're waiting on the men."

"I'll do it, if you'll show me where you keep everything."

"Great. Thank you, Wilma."

Cheryl thought again how nice it would be to have another woman around, as they walked back to the main house. Someone to help with the baby, visit with, talk with…

Yes, it would be nice, and she could hardly wait for them to move in.

CHAPTER NINE

Cheryl drove into town right after breakfast the next morning. Since Wilma had told her they hadn't kept anything from their last place, she decided to purchase a few more things to put around the dawdy haus to make it look cozy. A nice plant for the kitchen, maybe? And a couple of pretty pictures or knick-knacks from the dollar store over on Main. Maybe even a rug for the living room…

She glanced in the rearview mirror at Rebecca. Her car seat was still rear facing, but a small mirror fastened to the headrest meant she could always keep an eye on her.

"What do you think, Boo? Do you want to do a little shopping today?"

Rebecca gurgled happily and waved her doll in the air. "Ma-ma-ma."

Cheryl laughed and turned her gaze back to the road. "I'll take that as a yes." She frowned as she made a turn off of the main street. "I hope we can find some nice things for the Dormans. They seem like such a nice family. Didn't you think so? You liked Wilma, didn't you?"

She tossed another quick glance at Rebecca, but she was so absorbed in her toy, she didn't notice. Her phone rang, and Cheryl glanced at the car's media display, smiling as she saw who it was. Fortunately, she was just about to pull into Weaver Lumber, so she hit the answer button on her steering wheel and pulled into a parking spot.

"Morning, Momma."

"Morning, sugar. What are you up to today?"

"A little shopping with Rebecca." Cheryl shut off the engine and slid her keys into the pocket of her purse. "We've got a family moving into the dawdy haus so I came into town to pick up a few things."

"Some more people already? I thought you were going to wait a little while."

Briefly, Cheryl explained about the Dormans. "Pastor Lory said they've had a pretty hard time of it lately, with Kyle losing his job and all. Levi and I talked, and we both would like to help them out if we can."

"Well, I'm excited for you, sugar. The Lord is certainly going to bless you and Levi for your willingness to open up your home."

"Thanks, Momma. How is Daddy doing?"

There was a long pause, followed by, "Well, not so good. That's why I'm calling."

Cheryl's heart thumped. This was one of the hard things about being twenty-four hundred miles away from her parents. "Why? What happened? Is it serious?"

"Hold on now, it's nothing to get worked up over. He hurt his knee is all."

"Hurt his knee, doing what?"

"He twisted it stepping out of his truck into a pothole. At first, he kept saying it wasn't too bad but now, well, I thought you should know I'm taking him to the hospital later this week for an MRI."

"Uh-oh. Dad hates hospitals. Is it that serious?"

"I think so." Concern edged her mother's voice. "It's been giving him a lot of pain and there is quite a bit of swelling, even though we've been putting ice on it every day."

Cheryl started to speak, but her mother interrupted before she could.

"I know what you're going to ask, and the answer is yes, we've already been to our family doctor. He ordered a CT scan and couldn't find anything wrong, so we're thinking it might be a torn tendon."

"Oh no." Cheryl glanced at Rebecca in the mirror. She was still happily playing. "Momma, that's pretty serious. Should I talk to Levi about flying to Seattle?"

Her mother laughed. "Well, you know I would love to see you and that precious grandbaby of mine, but I don't think it's necessary. I can take care of your daddy for now. But maybe later, after we see what the MRI says..."

She trailed off, and Cheryl heard a note of worry in her voice. Both of her parents were getting older, and if her father had to have surgery, her mother would certainly need help caring for him, especially if he was laid up for a while.

She took a deep breath and lifted her chin. "Don't worry, Momma. We'll work it out. Just let me know what you hear, and we'll go from there."

Relief vibrated over the airwaves. "I'll do that, sugar."

"Gamma?" Rebecca's head lifted, as though she were just now realizing that her grandmother was on the phone.

"Yes, it's Grandma," Cheryl said, twisting in the seat to peek at Rebecca over the side of her car seat. "Can you say 'hi'?"

"Hi, Gamma!"

"Hello, Boo. How's Grandma's baby girl?"

Her mother's sweet Southern voice melted like warm honey over Cheryl. For a while, she smiled just listening to Rebecca trying to converse with her grandmother. Finally, she pulled off her seat belt and reached for her purse.

"Well, we'd better get inside, Momma. Please tell Daddy we'll be praying for him."

"I will. Give Rebecca a kiss for me and give my love to Levi."

"Will do. Bye, Momma. Love you."

"Love you too, sugar. Bye."

Cheryl reached for her purse and dropped her phone into one of the inside pockets. It was times like these that she hated living so far from her parents. It would be so nice just to be able to pop in and drop off a meal, or clean the bathrooms, basically just be there for her aging parents.

From the back seat, Rebecca let out a fussy whine.

"Okay, okay. I'm coming," Cheryl said, reaching for the door handle.

Through the windshield, she caught a glimpse of something shiny. A tall, lanky boy stood a few yards away, the sun glinting off one of the buckles of his leather backpack. From his profile, he looked like Zach. What was he doing standing around outside of Weaver's?

Cheryl watched for a second and then felt disgusted with herself for spying on a teenager.

"It's none of your business what he's doing," she chided herself. He could just be waiting for a friend, or maybe he was expecting a ride. She climbed from the car and reached into the back seat to pull Rebecca from her car seat. By the time she got her unbuckled and tugged the diaper bag from its spot on the floor, she fully expected Zach to be gone. Only he wasn't. Someone else had joined him. Someone who looked an awful lot like Blake.

Cheryl brought Rebecca to her hip and squinted over the top of the car at the boys. They were obviously talking, but how did Blake know Zach if he'd just moved to the area?

Suddenly, Blake's head swiveled in her direction, and Cheryl flinched self-consciously. Certain she'd been caught staring, she slammed the door shut and hugged Rebecca close. But instead of zeroing in on her, Blake turned back to Zach and held out his hand.

She squinted harder. He passed something to Zach, but from this distance, it was impossible to make it out. Zach jammed the object into this pocket and then switched hands and gave something back to Blake.

Cheryl instinctively gave Rebecca a squeeze. Had she just witnessed a drug deal? Was Blake buying drugs from Zach?

Her heart pounded as Blake spun and walked away. A second later, Zach left in the opposite direction. Cheryl bit her lip as she hiked her purse onto her shoulder and carried Rebecca into the lumber store. Whatever she'd just witnessed, it certainly looked fishy. She had to tell Levi. They couldn't let Blake bring drugs into their home, if that was indeed what he'd been about.

She settled Rebecca into the seat of a shopping cart and pulled her snack cup from the diaper bag to keep her occupied.

Then again, she thought, her mind quickly switching back to what she'd just seen, she couldn't accuse Blake of buying drugs without proof.

Cheryl's steps quickened through the store, her shoes clicking soundly against the cement floor. She'd planned on selecting a couple of plants for the dawdy haus, so she hurried to the garden center and plunked a small potted spider plant and a large hanging ivy in the shopping cart before returning to the checkout.

Once she'd paid for the plants, it only took her a few moments to snug Rebecca back into the car and drive the short distance to Hoffman's Furniture. Fortunately, the store was not busy, and Henry spotted her the moment she stepped through the doors. Cheryl lifted her hand to him, and he tucked his clipboard under his arm and made his way through the sets of living room furniture toward her.

"Good morning, Mrs. Cheryl. Are you here about the furniture delivery?" He flipped through the pages on his clipboard. "It is still early yet. I do not show the furniture being delivered until this afternoon, but if you need me to move it up I could—"

"No, no, Henry, that's all right."

Rebecca tugged on Cheryl's hand, so she let her go and watched as she scrambled onto a plush armchair.

"I'm...um...I'm not here about the furniture delivery," Cheryl continued. "To be honest, I came to ask you about something else, if you don't mind."

"Oh. I see." Henry slid the clipboard back under his arm, relief evident on his face. "Of course, Mrs. Cheryl. How can I help you?"

She sucked in a deep breath. "Well you see, Henry, it's about Zach, the boy Esther was talking to in the store the other day?"

He drew his shoulders back and nodded warily. "Ja."

Cheryl eased over to Rebecca and took hold of one of her hands to keep her from jumping on the chair and bouncing herself over the arm. "You said something the other day that worried me. I really feel like I need to look into it."

Henry's mouth remained tightly clamped, so she swung Rebecca into her arms and stepped toward him. "You said he was known for causing trouble but you didn't explain what kind. Was it drugs?"

His hand rose to the bruise on his eye. The color had faded some, but it still looked painful. He rubbed it gingerly then shook his head. "I am sorry, Mrs. Cheryl. I would like to help you, but I cannot. Esther was right to point out the error of my ways. I should not have spoken badly of Zachary without proof, no matter how worried I am about her."

A look of sharp pain flashed across his face, one he quickly hid by ducking his head. Though she wanted to press, Cheryl knew it would not do any good. The Amish did not approve of gossip, which was apparently how Henry now viewed any talk about Zach.

Rebecca let out a small whimper. Patting her back to soothe her, Cheryl nodded. "I understand, Henry," she said quietly.

He jerked his head up then winced and touched his finger to his eye.

"Still sore, huh?" She tipped her head toward the bruise.

"A little," he admitted with a grimace.

"You really should get it checked, Henry. You might have broken something."

"Nothing except my pride," he muttered wryly. "God's lessons can be painful sometimes."

"*God's* lesson, hmm?"

Rebecca reached for Henry's hair, and Cheryl quickly pulled her hand back.

"Henry, won't you tell me what happened to your eye? I know it must have something to do with Esther," she prompted.

Misery twisted his features, but he did not acknowledge her question one way or the other.

Cheryl blew out a resigned sigh. "All right. I won't pester you about it anymore. But I do hope you know you can talk to Levi and me if you need to. If we can be of any help at all, you just need to ask."

His gaze drifted toward the large window facing the street. No, it faced the Swiss Miss. His thoughts had drifted to Esther.

Cheryl's heart warmed as she watched him. "You really do care for her, don't you?"

He blinked in confusion then turned his gaze back to her. "I'm sorry, did you say something, Mrs. Cheryl?"

She pressed Rebecca's squirming body close and shook her head. "It was nothing. I'll talk to you later. Thanks for your help."

He nodded and motioned with the clipboard. "Let me know if the furniture does not arrive on time. I will look into it for you."

"I'm sure it will be fine. Bye, Henry."

"Bye, 'enry," Rebecca echoed, wriggling her chubby fingers at him and laughing.

A smile lifted the corners of his mouth as he waved back. Cheryl shook her head sadly. He was such a nice boy, perfect for Esther and so much better than—

Cheryl cut the thought short before it could form. She had no right to assume she knew Esther's mind.

She stopped. On the other hand, Esther had asked her to help prove Zach's innocence. If she happened to uncover a few unsavory details about him along the way, well, that was hardly her fault.

She pushed out the door of Hoffman's but instead of turning for her car, Cheryl headed across the street. It was high time she learned what had happened at that singing, and if Henry wouldn't tell her, well, she knew exactly who would.

Chapter Ten

Only a couple of customers trickled through the aisles inside the Swiss Miss, baskets slung over their arms as they browsed the handcrafted Amish goods. Mornings were typically slow, but that would change when the first tour bus arrived. Fortunately, that was still over an hour away, plenty of time for Cheryl to find out what happened to Henry's eye.

She grabbed an Amish doll to keep Rebecca occupied and went in search of Esther. She found her in the office, sorting through the inventory lists and making notations next to the items she needed to order. Cheryl knocked softly on the door and then poked her head inside.

"Hey, Esther. Do you have a minute?"

Esther lifted her head. Spotting Rebecca, she smiled and stuck out her arms. "I always have time for my sweet niece. Oh, and you too. Come on in, Cheryl," she said with a laugh.

Rebecca nearly dove across the desk into Esther's outstretched arms. Over and over, she repeated, "Et-ther, Et-ther," patting poor Esther's cheeks and tugging on the strings of her prayer kapp.

Finally, Esther pushed the inventory logs aside and settled Rebecca on the desk before resuming her seat. "So, what are you two doing in town?" she said, looking up from tickling Rebecca's belly.

"Shopping for the dawdy haus." Cheryl sank onto the chair across from Esther's. "The Dormans didn't bring a lot with them, so I thought I would pick up a few things to make it a little more homey."

Esther nodded her approval. "That is so nice, Cheryl. Do you want to pick out a couple of things from the store?"

"Just the doll."

Cheryl pointed at the toy waving precariously in Rebecca's hand. Leaning forward, she snatched it away before she could bonk Esther on the head with it. Rebecca let out a howl, and Cheryl plucked her from the desk and set her on the floor with the doll to quiet her.

"But that's not really why I came to see you," Cheryl continued, once Rebecca was mollified.

Instead of the eager nod that Cheryl expected, Esther fidgeted with the pencils on the desk, the tips making clicking noises against the top. That and Rebecca's happy babbling were the only sounds.

"Is this about our talk down at the pond? Normally, I would say yes," she continued quickly, "but the tour bus should be arriving soon."

"Actually, this is about the singing. I won't keep you long," she assured her gently.

Esther nodded and folded her hands in her lap. "All right. I guess I have a little time."

"Good." Cheryl placed her hands on the desk and laced her fingers. "I just left Hoffman's. Esther, do you have any idea what happened to Henry's eye? Did he and Zach have a fight?"

Esther pushed back from the desk. "Is that what he told you?" she asked sharply.

"Actually, he wouldn't tell me anything," she said quickly. "That's why I'm asking you."

Blowing out a breath, Esther eased out from behind the desk and paced from one end of the room to the other.

"It was his own fault," she said, agitation making her words crisp. "I told him to mind his own business. He should have listened to me. Perhaps then, things like this wouldn't happen."

"Things like what?" Cheryl pressed.

Esther slowed and pressed her hands to her stomach. "Henry and Zach got into an argument."

Cheryl scratched her head in disbelief. "About what? Henry is so quiet. He doesn't seem like the type to argue."

"You don't know Henry as well as I do, Cheryl. He wouldn't back down, and Zach got so angry. I mean, Henry practically forced Zach to punch him."

"Wait." Cheryl held up her hand. "Zach was *forced* to resort to violence? What are you talking about, Esther? That isn't the Amish way at all."

"I know that, of course, but Zach is Englisch. What was he supposed to do? He told Henry to turn around and walk away, but he wouldn't listen, so Zach—"

"What were they arguing about, Esther?" Cheryl interrupted. "Why was Henry so dead set against leaving?"

Though she suspected she knew the answer, she still wanted to hear it from Esther's own lips. She tapped the top of the desk, bidding Esther to sit. When she did, Cheryl leaned forward and looked her steadily in the eyes. "Well?"

"Zach asked me to go for a walk," she began, lifting her chin defensively. "There's nothing wrong with going for a walk. Henry had no business trying to stop us."

"No, there's not," Cheryl said, "but maybe you should back up a little. What was Zach doing at the singing in the first place?"

Esther squirmed on the chair and finally leaned forward earnestly. "I invited him, but only because he has been asking so many questions about our faith. I thought this would be a good way to introduce him to some of our ways."

She was trying to justify her actions, but that was a topic for another time. Cheryl returned her thoughts to Henry. "Okay, so Zach wanted you to go for a walk. Then what happened?"

Esther angled her chin angrily. "Henry saw us talking and barged in. I told him I didn't need his permission, that Zach and I were perfectly capable of making our own decisions, but Henry just kept insisting."

Cheryl shook her head, perplexed. "What was Henry insisting?"

Esther dropped her gaze, acting for the first time as though she were a little embarrassed. "Zach wanted the two of us to leave the singing alone. Henry said it was after dark and it wasn't proper. It wasn't really after dark. It was only about eight thirty or so," she argued.

Cheryl took her time mulling her words. "Esther, I thought you said you and Zach were just friends."

"We are." She gave a half-hearted shrug and then ducked her head. "I don't know. Maybe it is something more. But it wasn't Henry's place to poke his nose in. And then Zach got upset and told him to mind his own business or he'd have to teach him a lesson."

"And? What did Henry say?"

She gave a derisive snort. "He just kept repeating 'two cannot quarrel when one will not.'"

"Is that an Amish saying?"

She nodded.

"Well, Esther, that is the Amish way. You know it is against the church's teaching to fight, even in defense of oneself. In fact, standing on the outside looking at the situation, you could even say that Henry's actions were much more mature and respectful than Zach's."

Esther's brows drew together, and she bunched her hands on top of the desk angrily. "I knew you would take Henry's side."

"I'm not taking sides," Cheryl replied gently. "I'm just pointing out that it takes a much bigger man to refuse to fight than it does to give in to temptation."

Esther pushed to her feet, her shoulders thrust back stubbornly. "Zach is a nice guy, Cheryl. I really think if you gave him a chance, you would see that."

"I want to give him a chance, Esther, but so far, everything you've told me makes me think something else. And then today—"

She broke off and looked at Rebecca.

"What? What happened today?" Esther said, her brown eyes rounded and wide.

Cheryl shrugged and went to pick up Rebecca. "I saw him talking to someone, the boy whose family is moving into the dawdy haus."

"Blake? That's easy. They both play football. Zach was probably talking to him about practice or something like that."

Cheryl glanced at her in surprise. "I didn't realize you knew Blake."

She nodded and motioned around the store. "He came in here the other day with a few other guys."

"Okay, well I suppose they could have been talking about practice," Cheryl said, though deep down, she didn't think so. The conversation she had witnessed looked like something else entirely. She brushed the dust off Rebecca's clothes and then did the same to the doll and tucked it under her arm.

"We'd probably better be going. The tour bus should be stopping by soon, and I don't want to keep you."

"Okay." Esther followed her to the office door and stopped. "Cheryl, you do remember what you said about helping me prove Zach's innocence before you say anything to my parents, right?"

"That's not exactly how it went, but yes, I remember." Cheryl wagged her finger at Esther playfully. "I'll hold up my end of the bargain. I'll do what I can to find out who the marijuana belonged to, but you have to hold up your end too. Remember? Be open with your parents about Zach, Esther. I really think you'll regret it if you're not."

Her mouth turned down in an exasperated scowl, but she nodded. "Okay. Thanks, Cheryl. I'll see you later."

The door closed behind her with a solid click. Cheryl blew out a sigh. Much as she wanted to, she couldn't force Esther to talk to her parents. But maybe she wouldn't have to. Maybe all she had to do was prove to Esther who Zach really was. But then, who was he? A nice guy with a troubled past, or a troublemaker with a penchant for drugs?

Either way, Cheryl knew she had her work cut out for her.

CHAPTER ELEVEN

If Cheryl wanted to prove that Zach didn't bring drugs into the store, then she would have to find out who did, and that wouldn't be easy since she hadn't been in the store when they were left. She could ask around, of course, but one thing she had learned since she started volunteering with the youth group at church was kids didn't often like telling on each other.

She sighed as she climbed the stairs to the youth room for the Wednesday night service. Apparently, "nobody likes a narc," the old saying from her high school days, still applied.

A chorus of, "Hi, Mrs. Cheryl," greeted her as she entered the youth room. Several junior and senior high students crowded around the worship band, Bethany and Kelly among them. Bethany sometimes sang with them, so Cheryl wasn't surprised to see her warming up with a mike. But Kelly was hunched over a guitar, gently plucking at the strings and tuning it.

Cheryl walked over to her, smiling. "Hey there. I didn't know you played."

Kelly's head lifted, and she grinned. "Matthew has been teaching me." She pointed to one of the boys in the worship band.

Cheryl nodded and patted her shoulder. "That's awesome, Kelly. I'll let you warm up."

"Okay. Thanks, Mrs. Cheryl."

Over by the door, a group of boys had gathered, most of them football players, and Cheryl was glad to see that Blake was among them. Though he hung around the fringes and wasn't actively involved in the conversation, he was listening and nodding every so often. Could it be that what she had witnessed between him and Zach really had been about football? She hoped so.

As she watched, Blake's phone slid from his jacket pocket and landed with a soft thud on the carpeted floor, but because of the noise of the band warming up and the general chatter all around, he remained oblivious to it. Cheryl cringed as he took a step back. If he wasn't careful, he was going to step on it.

She hurried over toward him. "Blake, watch out. You're going to step on your phone."

His back remained turned toward her. Even this close, he couldn't hear her. Shaking her head, she bent and picked up the phone. Working with kids was anything but quiet.

She reached out to tap Blake's shoulder, but as she did, the phone vibrated in her other hand. Cheryl glanced at it in surprise. The display was lit up, and a text message from someone named Steven flashed across the top of the screen. And she was right, she noted. It was an iPhone. The latest model, which meant it was expensive.

"Blake." Cheryl nudged his arm with the phone. He turned to look at her. "You dropped this."

"Oh." He took the phone and slid it back into his coat pocket. "Thanks."

"You're welcome. Glad to see you here."

He gave a small nod. Someone tapping on the microphone drew their attention. The youth minister, Andrew, began the welcome by lifting his hands and urging everyone to their seats while the worship band played quietly behind him. Blake shot her a look, and Cheryl motioned for him to join the others heading toward the chairs.

Levi had also entered the youth room, so Cheryl took a seat by him and settled back to listen to Pastor Andrew deliver the lesson. She liked him. He was fun and imaginative, and the kids enjoyed his antics, but he always prepared well and delivered a strong message. Tonight was no different. Several of the students remained in prayer long after he finished, though Cheryl couldn't help but notice that Blake was not among them. He moved off to one side of the room and took out his phone while she and Levi split up to walk around the room and pray with those kids who asked.

When the prayer time concluded, pizza and drinks followed. Levi went to collect Rebecca, and Cheryl stayed to help serve the food. It was always a blessing, seeing the kids talk and fellowship together. Plus, it often gave her insight to what was happening at the school. Today she listened extra hard in hopes that she might catch wind of something that would help her uncover who at the school might have brought drugs into her store. Most of the talk centered around idle chatter, however—things like who was seeing who, and which girls were trying out for cheerleader, or which boys would make the football team. Before long, Cheryl had lost interest in the conversations and focused instead on cleaning up the kitchen after the meal.

"He said his name was Steven."

Cheryl pulled her hands from the sink full of soapy water she'd been using to wipe down the counters and rinse out the drink pitchers.

Another voice, this one stronger and higher pitched, drifted into the kitchen. "What was he doing at football practice?"

"How should I know? He said he was a friend of Blake's."

"The new guy?"

"Uh-huh."

Cheryl stuck her head out the kitchen door to see where the voices were coming from. Several girls were clustered around a couple of the football players. All of them were so busy talking, they paid no attention to her.

"All I know is, he was super cute," one of the girls said.

Her friend gave a disgusted snort and nudged her in the ribs. "Get a grip, Heather. He's like, ten years older than you."

"What? I just said he was cute."

Steven. The same Steven who had been texting Blake? Cheryl bit her lip and ducked back inside the kitchen. What was a much older man doing texting a high school boy?

Thoughts ran rampant inside Cheryl's head as she pondered the question.

"Hey, Cheryl. Are you ready to go?" Levi poked his head into the kitchen, a sleeping Rebecca cradled in his arms.

She nodded and hung the dishtowel over the cupboard door to dry. "Yep. All done in here. Just let me turn off the lights and lock up. I'll meet you out front."

Levi nodded and disappeared out the door. When she finished in the kitchen, Cheryl went in search of Andrew to let him know they were leaving, then joined her husband in the parking lot. It was long past time that she filled him in on what was happening, Cheryl decided as she climbed into the truck. She fastened her seat belt then turned in the seat to look at her husband. Fortunately, Rebecca was still sleeping, so she used the time it took to drive home to tell Levi everything, including the altercation that had led to Henry getting a black eye.

"So?" she finished, sagging back against the seat. "What do you think? Should I tell Naomi what has been going on with Esther?"

Levi thought a long moment, his fingers drumming against the steering wheel. "I think Esther is no longer a child. She is a young woman who will need to make her own choices."

Cheryl stared at him, open-mouthed, in the dim glow cast by the dashboard. "That was *not* what I expected you to say at all."

He shot a wry grin at her. "Why? You thought I would still think of Esther as my little sister?" He sobered and returned his attention to the road. "Well, you are right. I do. But at her age, it would be wrong of me to treat her as such. It is our duty to hold her accountable, but as a sister in Christ, and not as a young child."

Cheryl thought on this in silence. Finally she let out a heavy sigh. "You're right. But Naomi is more than just my mother-in-law. She's my friend. Don't I owe it to her to tell her what is going on?"

Levi took one hand off the steering wheel to squeeze her fingers. "I think your first instinct was right. Let Esther tell her when the time is right. In the meantime, you keep doing what you are doing—encourage her to tell the truth. Urge her to be straightforward in her dealings with Maam and Daed, but leave the rest to the Holy Spirit. It is His job to convict His people of wrongdoing, not ours."

With the air finally cleared between them, Cheryl found she could breathe easier, like a weight truly had been lifted from her chest. She sagged against the seat and nodded. "You're right. Thank you, Levi."

In reply, he brought her hand to his lips and pressed a quick kiss to her fingers. Cheryl's heart instantly melted. Pulling a tissue from her purse, she dabbed a swell of sudden tears from her eyes. What a precious gift she had been given in this godly man! If only Esther could be convinced to desire the same.

She lowered her hand, thinking. Perhaps she *could* be convinced, with the right evidence, of course.

Cheryl turned her gaze out the darkened passenger-side window. The tricky part would be getting Esther to listen, but she would have no choice if she were faced with concrete proof of Zach's actions. But how to get close enough to see what he was doing? That was going to take some thought, and more than a bit of divine assistance.

Chapter Twelve

Beau sat quietly on the windowsill, the tip of his tail swaying lazily back and forth as he gazed out over the farm. Cheryl watched him through narrowed eyelids, debating whether to get up or try and catch a few extra minutes of sleep. The baby's cry quickly settled the question.

Flipping back the covers, Cheryl sighed. Sleeping in was a thing of the past with a toddler in the house.

"I'm coming, Boo."

Rebecca's cries faded to playful chatter, so Cheryl pushed her fingers through her hair and staggered toward the bathroom. She had just enough time to wash her face and brush her teeth before Rebecca took up crying again. She hurried to lift her from her crib, then washed her face and changed her diaper before carrying her to the kitchen for breakfast.

Levi had already been up for a couple of hours. His breakfast dishes were rinsed and stacked neatly in the sink, and his coffee cup sat next to the coffee machine, a light brown stain in the bottom. Cheryl flipped the switch on the pot back to On as she passed then went to grab a box of cereal from the cupboard. The box felt light. She gave it a shake. There would be just enough for Rebecca's breakfast, but she would need to add more to her grocery list.

A milky mess later, Cheryl tossed the last of the breakfast dishes into the dishwasher and then went to clean up and dress before the Dormans arrived. Wilma had called and said the hotel was willing to refund some of their money if they moved out today, which wasn't a problem since the furniture Cheryl had ordered had been delivered and set up without a hitch. And the personal touches she'd added really made the house feel like a home—at least, she hoped Wilma would think so.

Just around the time Cheryl was putting the finishing touches to her makeup, an old pickup truck rumbled up the driveway. Cheryl grabbed her powder brush from Rebecca's hand and put it back in the cosmetics bag and then swung little Boo onto her hip before heading out to meet the Dormans.

Kyle stepped from the truck, the door squealing on rusty hinges as he banged it shut behind him. A smile spread across his face as he lifted his hand to greet her. "Morning, Mrs. Cheryl."

"Oh, just Cheryl, please." She offered a shy smile as she crossed the yard to meet them. "Can I help you with your things?"

"Thanks, but we've got it." Kyle rocked back onto his heels and stretched his arms wide. "Man, we sure are glad to have found a place to stay. That hotel was getting a little cramped."

Cheryl laughed. "I bet so."

"We really can't thank you and Levi enough for letting us stay," he continued. "Seriously. Thank you so much."

"You're very welcome."

Blake and Wilma climbed from the truck and circled around to join them. Blake had a large, olive-green duffel bag slung over his shoulder, but nothing else. Wilma lifted two battered suitcases from the bed of the truck and tottered toward them, one in each hand.

"Do you need help?" Cheryl bent to set Rebecca down, but Wilma quickly bade her wait.

"No, no," she said, giving a nod toward Rebecca. "You've got the baby. Besides, they're not heavy."

Kyle motioned toward the truck. "I'll grab the boxes. Blake, help your mother and then come on back and give me a hand, would you?"

Blake grunted and his brows lowered in a scowl, but he wasted no time dropping his bag in the entrance of the dawdy haus and returning to the truck to help his father unload the rest. As Wilma had said, it truly wasn't a lot, and the job was completed in just a few minutes.

Cheryl gestured toward the main house. "Have you had breakfast yet? I can put on a fresh pot of coffee and scramble up some eggs if you'd like."

"Oh no." Wilma smoothed her hair behind her ear nervously. "You don't have to do that. We wouldn't want to put you out."

"Besides, I'd really like to get started helping out your husband." Kyle's head swiveled as he looked around the farm. "If you'll just point us in his direction so he can put me and Blake to work?"

At the mention of his name, Blake stiffened and slanted a pointed look at his mother. "I have football practice this morning," he said, voice low. "Two-a-days started this week. I'm already behind."

"Already?" Cheryl tucked Rebecca's grasping fingers into hers and smiled. "School hasn't even begun yet."

"No, but practice usually starts before school does," Wilma explained, shooting an apologetic smile in the direction of her son.

"I'm sure the coach will understand," Kyle said firmly. "We've got one vehicle, and I can't take time to drive you to practice every day."

Cheryl averted her gaze. The glare Kyle gave his son could only be described as quelling.

"If it would help, I could take him," she began carefully. The gears in her head churned as the seed of an idea took root. "I often run by the school on my way to the store." She explained about the Swiss Miss and how she tried to get there several times a week just to see how things were going.

"Kyle?" Wilma urged, her voice almost a whisper.

She leaned over and plucked her husband's sleeve. Blake stood stoically beside her, refusing to even look at his father. Instead, he kept his gaze fixed on his dusty tennis shoes.

Finally, Kyle cleared his throat and shrugged. "I suppose that wouldn't hurt, if it's not any trouble."

"No trouble at all. I've got a few groceries I need to pick up." Cheryl bounced Rebecca playfully to keep her from squirming. And it would give her a chance to see if her idea would really work. She looked at Blake. "I'm going over there in just a few minutes, if you'd like to come."

Blake didn't wait for his father's reply but nodded and whirled toward the house. "I'll grab my stuff."

"Blake." Kyle stopped him with a firm tone. He waited until Blake scowled at him over his shoulder. "Come straight home after practice so you can help me and Mr. Miller with the farm. Understood?"

"Yeah, I got it." The door swung shut behind him as he disappeared in the house.

Kyle's mouth turned in an apologetic smile as he looked at Cheryl. "Teenagers. Sorry about that."

She shook her head. "Don't worry about it. I understand. My husband and I work with the youth at church, so we're pretty used to their moods."

"Well, anyway, thank you so much," Wilma said. "And you won't have to worry about picking him up after practice, or about taking him back this afternoon. I can take the truck after I finish unpacking our stuff. And I'll ask him to see about getting a ride home with one of the players tonight."

She sent a questioning glance at Kyle, who stood with arms crossed and nodded.

"That should be fine."

Cheryl smiled and jerked her thumb toward the door. "Good. Then I'll just run inside and finish getting Rebecca's things together. I'll only be a minute."

She hurried up the steps and set the baby on the floor to play while she packed her diaper bag. Trips into town were no longer simple, she thought as she grabbed her keys off the table. Now with a toddler in tow, even short trips meant diapers, and snack cups, and an extra change of clothes, just in case. Not to mention toys. She spent a frantic couple of minutes scouring the living room for Rebecca's favorite teddy and finally found it shoved between the cushions of the couch.

"Okay, here he is." She pushed the bear into Rebecca's waiting arms and then hoisted her and the diaper bag in one hand, and wrestled with the doorknob with the other. Surprisingly, Blake wasn't waiting next to her car as she'd expected. Cheryl deposited the diaper bag on the floor behind the driver's seat then buckled Rebecca into her car seat. Still no Blake. He couldn't have left without her. He didn't have a ride.

Cheryl started the car then turned the A/C to high. Odd as it seemed, he might have decided to wait for her at the dawdy haus. Frowning, she climbed from the car and went to check. She'd only gone a couple of feet when raised voices stopped her in her tracks. There was no mistaking the first voice or his tone. It was Kyle, and he wasn't happy. Blake's response was just as heated, though his voice was lower and more muffled. What were they arguing about?

Cheryl shifted her weight to one foot and drummed her fingertips nervously against her lips. Obviously, she couldn't leave Rebecca alone in the car, but she didn't like eavesdropping either and standing here torn by indecision qualified as just that.

"I said I've got to go! We'll talk about it when I get home from practice."

Suddenly, Blake rounded the corner of the house, Kyle hot on his heels. Both stopped dead at the sight of her.

"Um..." Cheryl blinked and jabbed her hand toward the car. "Are you ready to go?"

Blake strode to the car. "Yeah, I'm ready. Thanks, Mrs. Cheryl."

"You're welcome."

She punched the trunk release button on her key fob so Blake could dump his gym bag inside. Afterward, he jerked open the passenger door and climbed into the seat.

Cheryl puffed out a breath as she closed the trunk and then climbed in next to him. Kyle still watched silently from the corner of the dawdy haus, his hands jammed onto his hips and his face reddened.

"Everything okay over there?" Cheryl asked as she backed down the drive.

Blake shrugged, his face turned to the window. "Yeah. That's just the way my dad is, always upset about something."

Despite his words, he kept his fists pressed stiffly against his thighs, and one foot tapped in agitation against the floorboard.

She knew teenagers couldn't be coerced into talking about something they didn't want to. She waited, and hoped he'd open up if she didn't press.

Finally, he glanced over at her. "It's just... my dad can be pretty strict. We fight a lot, but it doesn't really mean anything."

She flashed an understanding smile. "I get that. I used to fight a lot with my parents too. It's all part of being a teenager."

"Yeah?" Blake gave a low grunt and sagged against the seat. "It seems like that's all my dad and I ever do."

Cheryl glanced sidelong at him, wishing she knew him better so she could read the look on his face. Was it anger or resignation or something else? She dragged her gaze back to the road. "Do you want to talk about it?"

He mulled the offer quietly for a long moment but then shook his head and turned his face back to the window. "Nah. Talking never really helps. Thanks anyway, Mrs. Cheryl."

His words struck a chord in her heart. There was so much loneliness and hurt to them. And yes, a bit of anger too.

Sugarcreek High School was an aging brick and glass structure with wide steps that led up to the main entrance. Behind it was the football practice field and a small field house, which was where Blake asked to be let off. Cheryl pulled around to the back of the school and then followed the signs and directional arrows until she arrived at the field house.

"Okay, here you go," she said, slipping the car into Park. She popped the trunk and then climbed out to close it once Blake removed his stuff.

He slung the gym bag over his shoulder then slid his free hand into his jeans pocket in the casual I-don't-care-what-the-world-thinks-of-me pose so many teenagers adopted. "Thanks again for the ride, Mrs. Cheryl."

She acknowledged his thanks with a wave. "It was no problem. Like I said, I pass right by here on my way to the store."

"Okay, well…" He shot a glance toward the field house where a few of the players were engaged in a rough game of keep-away with a player's jersey. "I'd better get over there. The guys told me coach's philosophy is if you're on time, you're late."

Cheryl cracked a smile. "That's funny. He must have been a military man. A guy I used to work with said the same thing. He was retired army," she explained.

Blake's expression showed only casual interest. "Maybe."

"Say, Blake?" Cheryl stopped him before he could turn to go. "Zach Waller is on the football team with you, right?"

He nodded and poked his thumb toward the field. "Uh-huh. He's the starting running back. I haven't seen him in action yet, but word is he's pretty good."

"So, then we should have a pretty good team this year."

He grinned. "I sure hope so."

Cheryl motioned toward the field. "Are all of the players required to be at two-a-days?"

"Unless the coach tells us otherwise. Sometimes they have special practices for just offense, or just defense, stuff like that."

She nodded. That meant Zach would be tied up for at least a couple of hours. Plenty of time for what she had planned. And afterward, she would look for opportunities to watch him unobserved.

"Gotcha." She waved. "Have fun at practice."

He snorted. "I'll try. See you later."

He took off with a wave and made his way toward the group of boys. Cheryl bumped the trunk closed and moved to climb back into the car, but struck by a sudden thought, she laid her hand on the roof and stopped. Blake didn't know any of those boys, except for maybe Zach. Asking for a ride from one of them would probably be hard.

"Hey, Blake?"

He turned back to look at her curiously.

"Feel free to call if it turns out you do need a ride home." She hurried to grab a slip of paper from her purse, scribbled down her number, and handed it to him. "Levi or I will be glad to come and get you."

For a long moment, he merely stared, as though her words had somehow taken him by surprise. Then, one of the other players yelled his name and signaled that it was time to run warm-up laps. Blake shoved the paper in his pocket, gave Cheryl a quick thumbs-up, and then took off at a run.

"I really hope it wasn't you," she whispered as she watched him jog across the practice field toward two long benches that were almost overrun with wild blackberry bushes.

The boys on the team gave the brambly bushes a wide berth, Blake included. Apparently, the school's recent budget cuts meant fewer men on the grounds crew. Not that it mattered much. This was the practice field after all.

"Momma, Momma!" Apparently tired of sitting still, Rebecca squirmed in her car seat and reached out to slap the window with her chubby hand.

"Okay, okay. Time to go check out my idea." Cheryl climbed into the car and backed it around so it pointed toward the high school. Catching Rebecca's eye in the mirror, she asked, "So, shall we go pay a visit to the principal?"

Rebecca's head bobbed, and her lips curled in a smile. Waving the teddy bear in one hand, she slapped at the window again, only this time, Cheryl had the distinct impression it was her way of saying, "Giddy up!"

CHAPTER THIRTEEN

Sugarcreek High School was an older building, but lovingly cared for. The floors gleamed with a coat of fresh polish, and all of the lockers had been scrubbed of graffiti and painted in the school's colors in preparation for the upcoming year. Even the classrooms looked eager, waiting to be filled with enthusiastic students yearning for friendship, or popularity, or graduation day.

Memories of her own high school days filled Cheryl's thoughts as she walked the long halls, pacing her steps to match Rebecca's smaller stride.

"One." Rebecca tapped a locker as they passed. "Two. One. Two. One."

"What comes after two?" Cheryl said, laughing.

"One! Pretty." Rebecca stopped and patted the floor, then continued walking, her words as disorganized and rambling as her steps.

Finally, they reached the block of offices for the administrative staff and secretary. Painted in gilded letters on the glass door were the words Daniel McKeller, Principal. Cheryl pushed it open and went inside.

A counter separated the entrance from the rest of the offices. A small black nameplate attached to one corner read "Receptionist" but no one was there to greet them. Cheryl lifted Rebecca into her arms and rang a small silver bell then moved aside to wait. Near the back of the office, a door opened and a woman with silver hair and wire-rimmed glasses approached.

"Well, good morning." She offered a bright smile to Rebecca and then scrunched her nose playfully when Rebecca smiled back. She turned her gaze to Cheryl. "Can I help you?"

"Hi. Good morning. My name is Cheryl Miller. Is Principal McKeller in?"

She shook her head apologetically. "Oh, no. Sorry. He's in Columbus this week attending a conference. But I'm Mrs. Spalding, his secretary. Is there something I can help you with?" She smiled and plucked at Rebecca's shoe. "Are we enrolling a new student?"

Cheryl laughed and ducked her head to see Rebecca's reaction. Though she watched Mrs. Spalding with interest, she didn't smile. Instead, she pulled her foot back and continued staring.

"Sorry. She can be shy sometimes."

"Oh, I know. I've got children and grandchildren of my own." She smiled and motioned toward Cheryl. "So, what can I do for you?"

"Well, I really just had a few questions about the school and students and so forth."

Mrs. Spalding's eyebrows rose. "Planning for this little one's schooling already? I'm impressed."

Cheryl laughed and hitched Rebecca higher on her hip. "No, that's not it. I'm organized but not that organized."

Mrs. Spalding laughed and released the latch on a part of the counter that flipped back to allow people through. She motioned

Cheryl and Rebecca inside then pointed toward the office from which she'd come. "Come on in and have a seat. I've got a few toys that I leave here for when parents come in with little ones. We'll let your daughter play while we talk."

"Oh, thank you. That would be nice."

Mrs. Spalding's office was neat and tastefully decorated. Along with a large, framed painting on one wall, family photos were scattered about, making the place seem homey and inviting. She disappeared into a closet of some sort near the back of the office and returned with a plastic bin filled with toys.

"Here we are." She set the bin down in front of Rebecca and then took out one of the plastic dolls and gave it a wiggle. "How about this one?"

Rebecca reached for it in response and then bestowed a large smile on Mrs. Spalding.

"You've got a friend for life now," Cheryl said, laughing.

"Aww, she's so sweet. I just loved seeing my grandkids at this age. They're all in their teen years now." Mrs. Spalding rose and circled around the desk to sit, then invited Cheryl to draw up one of the chairs opposite her. "So, what can I do for you?"

"Well..." Cheryl shot a glance at Rebecca, unsure how to begin. "I'm sure this is probably going to sound strange, but it's been quite a few years since I've been in high school, so I know I'm probably out of touch with the way things are now."

"What kind of things? Do you mean with technology?" She lifted her brows questioningly.

Cheryl shifted in her chair. "Not exactly, I'm afraid. I'm trying to understand where these students are socially. For example, kids didn't really do a lot of drinking and partying when I was in school. I mean, it went on some, but usually it was a small group of kids and everybody knew to stay away from those students. Now, listening to the youth group I work with over at Friendship Mennonite, it seems like it's a much bigger problem, so much that its even trickling over into the youth from plain families." She leaned toward Mrs. Spalding's desk. "Would you say drugs and alcohol are prevalent here in Sugarcreek? We're such a small town, I didn't really think so before, but now I'm not so sure."

To her shock—or perhaps a better word was to her sorrow—Mrs. Spalding hardly seemed surprised by her question. Her head bobbed sadly, her veined hands fidgeting with the buttons on her collared shirt.

"Things are very different nowadays, that's for sure. We've certainly seen a rising trend of children getting into trouble a lot younger than they used to, and in a wider variety of ways than say, ten or twenty years ago." She held up her finger. "But I wouldn't say we're very different from any of the surrounding schools. This is a widespread problem, not one that is particular to our area, or even our state."

Cheryl instantly recognized the tiny note of defensiveness in the woman's voice and took steps to alleviate it. "I completely understand what you're saying, Mrs. Spalding. I guess I should explain why I'm asking, so I don't give you the wrong idea about my coming here."

She told Mrs. Spalding about the store and the drugs that had been found there. "Officer Ortega seems pretty certain that they probably belonged to a student, but I was so surprised since nothing like that has happened there before."

Mrs. Spalding folded her hands on the desk and frowned. "I'm sad to hear about this. I've worked at this school for over thirty years. It used to be, we'd have a couple of cases a year of students being caught with drugs. Now, it seems to happen much more often."

"May I ask what the school's policy is when something like that happens?" Cheryl said.

"Of course." Mrs. Spalding rose and took a thin booklet from a shelf behind her desk. "It's all right here in our Student Code of Conduct." She scanned the table of contents and then flipped open to one of the pages. For some time, she read silently, nodding, and finally turned the book for Cheryl to see. "Paragraph four...right there."

Cheryl took the book and read where she indicated. "A person commits an offense (Class C misdemeanor) if the person possesses an intoxicating beverage for consumption, sale, or distribution while on the grounds or in the building of a public school." She lifted her head. "Is it the same for drug use?"

Mrs. Spalding nodded. "Keep reading."

Cheryl slid her finger down the page. "Oh, here it is. A person commits an offense (Class B misdemeanor) if the person inhales, ingests, applies, uses, or possesses an abusable volatile chemical."

"Our school board is quite strict on this policy."

"Do you mean others are not?"

Mrs. Spalding took the book back and returned it to its place on the shelf. "How should I say this... not always?" She shook her head in disgust. "Some school districts have been rumored to overlook these types of offenses when it affects one of their athletes. Not this one, mind you," she added quickly, "and none that I've worked for in the past. But unfortunately, it's not uncommon, and it's not just drugs. It's the same for test scores, misbehavior in class, that sort of thing."

Cheryl stared at her in disbelief. "Just so I understand, are you saying some districts let their students get away with those things simply because they don't want their team to lose?"

Mrs. Spalding adjusted her glasses and made a rolling motion with her hand. "Let me put it this way. School districts are made up of school boards, people who are elected to their positions every couple of years or so. Sometimes, the people in those positions have an agenda, and it's not always what's best for the students. Those people tend to hire based solely on winning records. And if a coach doesn't deliver?" She shrugged. "That kind of pressure can make people turn a blind eye."

"In other words, they do not encourage that behavior, but they aren't punishing students who engage in it."

She nodded sadly. "So, did Officer Ortega say why she thought the drugs you found belonged to a student?"

"Well, it was a relatively small amount," Cheryl explained, "and it was in a plain Ziploc bag. Plus, it looked like it had just fallen out of someone's pocket, so I guess she just assumed."

"I see." Mrs. Spalding blew out a breath and pressed her palms flat against her desk. "Well, like I said before, our little school isn't exempt from the problems plaguing most students nowadays. Even in a small town like this, we've seen a steady increase of drug and alcohol use just like everywhere else. It's sad, really. Makes me glad I'm getting close to retirement."

Cheryl certainly understood the sentiment. More than once, she'd wondered what kind of world her baby daughter would inherit. She scooped her up and held her close. Rebecca, however, wasn't happy to be taken from her toys and squirmed to get loose. Finally, Cheryl put her down.

Mrs. Spalding smiled. "She's an independent one. You'll have your hands full when she gets to be a teenager."

"Thank goodness I have lots of help," Cheryl said. "My mother and my mother-in-law are both very wise women."

"That's wonderful."

Cheryl nodded in agreement. "I am blessed." She paused and rested her hand on Mrs. Spalding's desk. "So, I have just one last question, if you don't mind."

Mrs. Spalding motioned for her to continue. "Go right ahead."

"I'm just curious, is there a teacher by the name of Steven on the faculty here? Possibly a coach or something?"

Mrs. Spalding didn't hesitate, but shook her head immediately. "Not that I'm aware of, though Coach Tanner does bring in some professional athletes to work with the kids from time to time. He knows a lot of former football players. He used to play for the Cleveland Browns. Of course, that was several years ago now."

"The NFL. Wow. He must be really good."

She nodded. "We're lucky to have him, and not just because of his talent. He really cares about his players."

Cheryl mulled that thought over in her head. The coach brought in football players to work with the team. Could that explain the man the girls from the youth group had seen? She nodded and moved to rise. "Okay, well, thank you so much for your time, Mrs. Spalding. I really appreciate your help."

She bent to pick up the toys, but Mrs. Spalding shooed her away with a smile.

"Oh, don't worry about those. I can take care of them." She waved around the office. "As you can see, we're not real busy around here this time of year, but wait until next week, when early registration picks up. It'll look like a whole different place entirely."

Cheryl laughed and stood. "I was a little surprised to find someone in the office. I thought maybe you closed for the summer."

"We're open off and on for things like summer school and make-up tests. Plus, students come by needing things like verification of enrollment for their driver's licenses and such. Usually, I take a couple weeks off in July, but since Mr. McKeller is out of town, I volunteered to keep the office open for him."

"Well, I'm glad I found you. Thanks again for your help."

"Oh, you're very welcome."

Mrs. Spalding gave Cheryl and Rebecca a cheerful wave as they let themselves out. Oddly, the halls didn't seem quite so bright after hearing what the secretary had to say. Cheryl hurried past the colorful lockers, a little sad but mostly anxious to get back to her safe little home on her quiet little farm.

Chapter Fourteen

Four hours.

Cheryl sprinkled one last teaspoon of garlic and rosemary over the second roasted chicken she was preparing for supper and then slid the roasting pan inside the steaming oven.

Four hours she'd spent following Zach around town, watching his every move, and all she'd learned was that he really liked cheeseburgers. He'd had one for lunch, stopped by a friend's house, and then went back for a second one right before he returned to practice.

She grimaced. She'd probably gained two pounds just thinking about what all that fat would do to her waistline.

She wiped her hands on a towel and glanced at the clock. It was early yet, only four thirty, but she had invited her in-laws over for supper and she wanted to be sure everything was ready by the time the men came in from working on the farm.

She shut the oven door and paused with the pot holder on the handle. Should she have invited the Dormans too? It wouldn't hurt to ask them, and it might even make them feel a little more welcome. She shook her head, chastising herself for not having thought of it earlier.

"Anyone home?" Naomi's voice drifted from the front door.

"In the kitchen," Cheryl called.

Rebecca was banging a spoon against the tray on her high chair. Naomi pressed a kiss to her head as she passed and then neared to give Cheryl a hug. Pulling away, she eyed Cheryl, then stuck her nose in the air.

"What is this I smell? Rosemary? Garlic?"

Cheryl laughed and tossed the pot holders onto the counter. "I'm trying out your recipe for roasted chicken. I was just about to invite the Dormans to join us. Do you think two chickens will be enough for everyone?"

Naomi patted the basket swinging from her arm. "Well, since I also brought a large bowl of potato salad and Elizabeth is coming with a homemade cherry crumble, I would say so."

Cheryl's mouth watered just thinking of Elizabeth's cherry crumble. She smiled broadly and opened the freezer door. "Good thing I bought ice cream."

Phones had not yet been installed in the dawdy haus, so Cheryl moved to the back door. "I'll go and speak to Wilma right now. Do you mind watching Rebecca for a moment?"

"Not at all."

Naomi set down the basket and went to give Rebecca a tickle under the chin. Cheryl smiled watching her interact with her grandchild. Not only did she play with her, she demonstrated love and patience in her teaching, habits Cheryl wanted to cultivate in her own heart. She left to invite the Dormans, thankful for the example God had placed in her life to help her raise her baby.

When she returned, Naomi was at the sink washing her hands and rinsing out Rebecca's bowl.

"Okay, that's settled," Cheryl said, closing the kitchen door behind her. "They'll be here at six. I also invited Wilma to Grace's baby shower. I thought it might be a good opportunity for her to get acquainted with some of the women from church."

"That was good thinking," Naomi said. She opened the cupboard. "So we will add three more plates at the table?"

"Actually, just two." Cheryl shook her head and pointed at the clock. "Blake won't be home from practice until around seven."

"So late." Naomi tsked and lifted the plates out of the cupboard. "All right. What can I help you do?"

"Do you want to be in charge of the salad while I fix up some green beans?"

"Of course." She nodded approvingly as she reached for a large wooden salad bowl from one of the top shelves in the cupboard. "You are becoming quite an accomplished cook."

Cheryl grinned wryly and took out a large pot for the green beans. "Well, I'm accomplishing cooking, but I'm not sure that's the same thing."

Naomi's laughter filled the kitchen—a pleasant sound and one Cheryl had grown to appreciate even more now that she and Levi were married. It was a special thing to have a mother-in-law she loved and respected, and one whose friendship she treasured. While they worked, Cheryl filled Naomi in on everything she'd learned from Mrs. Spalding at the school.

Naomi made a tutting sound as she listened. "I am very sad to hear this news. Of course, I am aware that things are very different for Englisch *kinder* than they are for the Amish. They are faced with a much wider array of challenges, what with computers, and television, and movies and the like. But to hear the problem is growing, well that is a troubling thing, for sure and for certain."

Maybe *not* so different. Cheryl felt her heart grow heavy thinking of the possibility that the things Naomi mentioned had affected even her own family. She bit her lip and stirred the pot of green beans absently while she debated whether or not to tell Naomi about the scene she'd witnessed between Blake and Zach, and later on, Blake and his father.

She tapped the spoon against the side of the pot and then laid it on a pretty ceramic spoon rest someone had given to her and Levi as a wedding present. "Naomi...um...speaking of troubling..."

Naomi looked up from the head of lettuce she'd been tearing into the salad bowl. "Ja, Cheryl?"

Cheryl pushed away from the stove and went to retrieve the spoon Rebecca had tossed onto the floor. "Naomi, you remember the drugs I found in the store the other day?"

Her hands stilled, and she nodded. "Ja. You have learned who they belong to?"

"Not yet, unfortunately, but I did see something the other day that worried me."

Briefly, Cheryl explained about the encounter she'd witnessed between Blake and Zach, but left out any explanation of who Zach was and his connection to Esther. Instead, she described him as merely "one of the boys from the football team." Still, lines of concern crept over Naomi's face as she listened.

She crossed to Rebecca's high chair and laid her hand on the back. "You do not think Blake is the one who brought the drugs into the store, do you?"

"To be honest, I'm not sure," Cheryl admitted. "But the more I learn about the Dormans, the more apparent it is that the family has troubles beyond just looking for a place to stay."

"Troubles? What kind of troubles?"

"Between Kyle and his son, I think."

Cheryl told her about the altercation she had witnessed and the effect it'd had on Blake. While she talked, Naomi went back to the sink and resumed tearing the lettuce, her hands moving absently in a quiet, steady rhythm.

"He definitely looked and sounded angry, but he seemed a little sad too, when he got in the car," Cheryl said. "I got the impression arguments between him and his father are a pretty common thing. I think they bother Blake a lot more than he let on."

Naomi remained silent for a long moment, washing tomatoes under the tap and giving a small shake of her head every now and then. At last, she shut off the water and turned to rest her hip against the sink.

"I am very glad that you and Levi have decided to take this family in."

"Really?"

Cheryl directed a quick glance at Rebecca, who was scooping up Cheerios with her spoon and dropping them on the floor for

Beau. But instead of gobbling them up, he sniffed at them disdainfully, his tail swishing.

She switched her gaze back to Naomi. "I was a little worried you might not approve."

Naomi set the tomato on the counter and took hold of Cheryl's hands. "'Be not forgetful to entertain strangers; for thereby some have entertained angels unawares.' This is what the Scriptures say, ain't so?"

"That is true, but..."

"But?" She loosed her hands and eyed her expectantly.

Cheryl fidgeted nervously as she mulled over the exchange she'd witnessed between Blake and Zach. Blake wasn't necessarily buying drugs. He could just as easily have been selling them to Zach, if there were drugs involved at all. She frowned and crossed her arms.

"What if it was Blake who brought the drugs into town? I mean, they showed up around the same time."

Naomi took her time answering. She picked up a corner of her apron and rubbed it over her hands in slow circles. When she spoke, it was in gentle, encouraging tones. "Going by what you say about this family's troubles, it sounds to me as though they could use a strong, godly couple to come alongside them and mentor them. And besides, did you not tell me that the secretary at the school said drugs were already a problem?"

Naomi's reassurance settled like a balm over Cheryl's spirit. She straightened and reached for the pepper to season the green beans. "You're right. If Blake is somehow mixed up with drugs, then he needs our help. I'll try and keep an eye on him."

And Zach too.

While supper finished cooking, she and Naomi set the table and prepared a couple of large pitchers of lemonade. Rebecca was too hungry and cranky to wait for supper, so Cheryl fed her and then laid her down for a nap before everyone arrived. A short while later, the door swung open and Levi stepped inside, followed closely by his brother Eli, and his father.

Seth poked his nose in the air and took a long whiff. "Something smells delicious." He narrowed his eyes playfully at Cheryl and stroked his long beard. "Is this your doing?"

"Believe it or not. Though I did follow Naomi's recipe pretty closely," Cheryl said with a smile.

Laughing, Seth moved to Naomi and gave her an affectionate hug. "Well, Wife, it looks as though your cooking skills have rubbed off on your daughter-in-law."

"Not even close," Cheryl protested, "but I'm learning."

She crossed to Levi, who dipped his head and gave her a peck on the cheek.

"Is Rebecca napping?"

"Uh-huh. I just laid her down. Did you see the Dormans?"

"Right behind us." He hitched his thumb toward the door. "Kyle said he was going to wash up and change, and they would be right over."

"Okay, good." Cheryl turned to take the chickens from the oven. "How did it go with Kyle today?"

"Goot," Levi said, crossing to the sink to wash his hands. "I like him."

Seth nodded in agreement. "He is a hard worker and a fast learner. He will be an asset to us come harvest time."

Cheryl slid an oven mitt over her hand. "I'm glad to hear it."

"Oh, here is Elizabeth and Esther." Naomi moved to open the door for the girls, then motioned to Seth and Levi. "Come, let us go into the dining room and get out of Cheryl's hair. Levi, grab the potato salad from the refrigerator."

There was laughter and collective groans, but Naomi ignored them and shooed everyone through the door then returned to pour the green beans into a large bowl and carry them to the table. A moment later, the front doorbell rang, and Cheryl heard Levi welcoming Kyle and Wilma. Grabbing a meat fork, Cheryl moved the roasted chickens onto a large serving platter then arranged some fresh parsley around them and followed Naomi into the dining room.

Wilma's eyes rounded at the sight of the steam rising from the golden roasted chickens. "Oh my goodness, that looks delicious." Circling to Cheryl's side, she added, "Is there anything I can do to help?"

"Well, if you wouldn't mind pouring the lemonade," Cheryl said, giving a tilt of her head toward the empty glasses.

Wilma hefted one of the pitchers from the sideboard. "Who wants lemonade?"

While she poured, Cheryl and Naomi put the finishing touches on the food and then they all settled down to pray. Cheryl's heart swelled listening to her husband's deep voice as he asked the blessing over the food. Praying aloud was different from the way her in-laws did it in their home, where the family prayed silently to themselves, but more than once, Cheryl had caught Seth watching Levi, his eyes shining with love and pride. Though she had not mentioned it to him, Cheryl felt exactly the same way— Levi's hushed voice, brimming with reverence, was a sound she knew she would never tire of, and one for which she would always give thanks.

The moment Levi said amen, the table erupted with chatter and many hands passing and reaching for the food. When the last plate was served, the conversation settled to talk of the farm and the work that had been done that day, and what would need to be done tomorrow. Kyle asked a lot of questions, mostly about the kinds of crops the Millers grew, but he also wondered about how they knew to rotate the planting so that no field ever became fallow, or how they knew when one of their animals was ailing. Levi and Seth took turns answering, both men patient in their explanations and inviting his curiosity with good humor.

Once the meal was finished, Esther offered to help clear the plates while Elizabeth went to fetch the ice cream and cherry crumble. Cheryl's phone rang, so she excused herself to go and see who was calling. The caller ID showed a number she didn't recognize. Normally she would have let it go to voice mail, but something inside prompted her to answer.

She lifted the receiver to her ear warily. "Hello?"

"Hello, Mrs. Miller? This is Coach Tanner calling from Sugarcreek High School. Blake Dorman gave me your number. Is Mr. or Mrs. Dorman available?"

"Coach Tanner?" Cheryl's heart thumped. Had something happened to Blake during practice? Was he hurt? She fumbled with the phone and almost dropped it. "Um...yes, Mrs. Dorman is right here. I'll go get her."

She set the phone on the hall table and ducked into the dining room to signal to Wilma. Concern showed on Wilma's face as she pushed back from the table and joined Cheryl in the hall.

"What is it? Is everything all right?"

"It's Coach Tanner," Cheryl said, handing her the phone. "He asked for you."

"Oh." The worry lines deepened on Wilma's brow. She glanced at the phone and then at Cheryl. "Did he say why he's calling?"

She shook her head and motioned toward Levi's office just off the front door. "You can step into the study if you like. It's quiet there. I'll go and start a pot of coffee while you talk to him."

"Thank you," she said and then pressed the phone to her ear, already talking as she ducked into the study. "This is Wilma Dorman."

Elizabeth had begun serving the cherry crumble, and Esther was scooping out the ice cream, when Cheryl returned carrying a carafe of coffee. She had just begun pouring the first cup when Wilma reentered the dining room, her face white, the phone clutched in both hands. Spying Cheryl, she crossed to her and handed her the phone.

"Thank you, Cheryl," she said, avoiding her gaze.

"Wilma, is everything all right?" she said quietly.

"Uh..."

Kyle's chair scraped back before she could answer. His gaze was stony as he jerked his head toward the hall. "Let's talk outside." He looked toward Levi. "Would you excuse us?"

At Levi's nod, he grasped his wife's elbow and walked with her toward the door.

Everyone's face registered the same surprise and concern Cheryl felt. Naomi looked at her, eyes wide.

"What has happened?"

Cheryl set down the carafe and shook her head. "I'm not sure. That was the football coach who called."

"Was Blake hurt during practice?" Levi said.

Cheryl shrugged. "He didn't say, and I didn't think I should ask."

"Ne, that would not have been goot," Seth said.

Next to him, Naomi nodded her agreement. "Maybe we should go—"

Just then the screen door screeched open, and Kyle and Wilma returned to the dining room.

"I'm so sorry," Kyle said, casting a look around the dining room. "I'm afraid we're going to have to cut this a little short."

"No problem," Cheryl said quickly, then paused, biting her lip. "Is everything all right?"

Kyle's gaze flicked to his wife. Wilma remained pressed to his side, her face sullen and eyes downcast. Slowly, he shook his head. "Actually, when you and Levi have a moment, Wilma and I would like to speak with you about Blake."

Seth braced his hands on the table and pushed upright. "We will go."

Kyle raised his hand. "Oh, we didn't mean—"

Seth shook his head firmly. "Ne, ne. It is all right. You need to talk, and Naomi and I do not wish to intrude. Please." He motioned them to the table. "Family is always more important than cherry crumble."

Everyone smiled at his generous attempt at lightening the mood, but Naomi was already fetching her black sweater from the hooks near the door and waving for Elizabeth and Esther to do the same. Eli rose when his father did and circled the table to stand by his side.

Seth gave a nod to Wilma, then thanked Cheryl for dinner and leaned forward to shake Kyle's hand. "We will see you tomorrow, Kyle."

"Of course. Bright and early."

"Goodbye, Cheryl." Naomi gave her a quick squeeze, one that conveyed her support and prayers. "Give Rebecca a kiss for us."

"I will." She followed the Millers to the door and waved as they went out, then returned to the dining room and her cooling pot of coffee. "Would anyone like a cup?" she said, holding it high.

Wilma was already seated at the table, as were Kyle and Levi.

"No, thank—" she began.

"Actually, that might be good," Kyle interrupted. He slid his cup toward Cheryl, motioning her hand away when she picked up the cream to offer him some. "No thanks. Black is good."

Levi leaned forward to rest his arms on the table. "So, what is all this about, Kyle? Is everything all right with Blake?"

Cheryl set the pot down quietly, glad her husband had taken the initiative and started the conversation.

Kyle laced his fingers around his cup, his knuckles white with strain. "I wish I could say yes, but honestly, I'm not even sure I know how to answer that question."

"What is it?" Cheryl asked. "What's going on?"

Kyle let out a heavy sigh, the kind she had often heard her parents make whenever they were worried about one of their kids.

"First things first, I suppose." He lifted his head and met Levi's gaze squarely. "I need to apologize to you for not being completely honest when we first met. You see, I wasn't laid off from my job in Wellington. I quit. And we didn't move because I was looking for work. We left because I wanted to get Blake away from the kids he was hanging around with."

Wilma had yet to speak. Cheryl shot her a glance. She still looked pale, but aside from that, her face was curiously devoid of emotion—worry or otherwise.

"What kind of kids?" Levi said, reclaiming Cheryl's attention.

"Bad kids. Kids with drug problems. The kind that like to party. We thought we were helping him by moving to a smaller town. We thought it would be harder for him to get into trouble."

Cheryl blew out a breath between narrowly parted lips. So, it *was* Blake's drugs she'd found in the store! And her hunch about the exchange she'd witnessed between him and Zach? That was probably right too.

"If young people are looking for trouble, they will always find it," Levi said quietly.

Kyle nodded glumly. "Yeah, I guess I know that now. It was silly of me to think a few miles would make a difference. But a person will do just about anything for their kids, you know?"

Next to him, Wilma made a sharp sound of pain, but she still refused to look up, just kept twisting her hands in her lap, round and round, over and under.

Pity for her filled Cheryl's chest. "Have you tried getting him some help?"

"We spoke to his counselor back in Wellington," Kyle said, "but it was actually hard to get anywhere there."

"What do you mean?"

"Well..." He lifted one shoulder in disgust. "Like we told you, Blake was All-State. Any time he got into the least bit of trouble, the coach there bailed him out."

"What?"

He nodded sadly. "It's true. That was one of the reasons we decided to leave. Our son's life was too important."

"Kyle." Wilma spoke sharply, her eyes narrowed and hard. He stared back for a long moment and finally broke his gaze with her to look at Cheryl and Levi.

"The truth is, we've disagreed over the best way to handle Blake. It was my idea to move here, not Wilma's. She thought moving him away from his friends would only make things worse."

He reached over and laid his hand over hers. She flinched. It was a small movement, almost imperceptible, but definitely there. Kyle pulled his hand away.

"Anyway, just now on the phone Coach Tanner told Wilma one of the boys claimed he saw marijuana in Blake's bag, but by the time he checked, the stash was gone."

"Gone?" Levi's brows bunched. "You mean he hid it?"

Kyle nodded. "Probably flushed it down the field house toilet, or tossed it into the woods behind the practice field."

Cheryl's curiosity piqued. "You know about the woods? I didn't realize you'd been by the practice field."

"Oh, yes, when we signed him up to play. We finally got clearance from his previous coach." Kyle spread his hands wide and blew out a long, lingering breath. "Anyway, now that you know the real reason why we're here, I have to ask if you've changed your minds about letting us stay. If you have, please know that we completely understand. We should have been forthcoming from the beginning, and we won't blame you a bit if you want us to leave."

Cheryl said nothing and looked at her husband. Levi sat with his hand cupping his chin, his fingers running over the short growth of beard. It was a movement very similar to the one Seth did when he was deep in thought.

Finally, he glanced at Cheryl, a question shining in the depth of his blue eyes. He wasn't asking her what they should do, he was seeking her support in speaking for them. She nodded, her heart thrilling at the mutual trust and shared confidence that existed between her and her husband.

Levi cleared his throat and leaned forward to clasp his hands on the tabletop. "It is true that we will need to discuss how best to handle this situation with Blake. I am sure you can understand that I cannot allow drugs to be brought onto my farm or into my home."

"Of course," Kyle said quickly, grasping the edge of the table in both hands and rising from his chair. "Like I said, if you want us to leave—"

Cheryl shook her head, and Levi held up his hand before he could finish.

"Ne. Please." He motioned for Kyle to sit down, then re-clasped his hands atop the table. "It is goot that you have been honest with us about Blake's problem. Maybe now, we will be able to help."

"You…want to *help* us?" Wilma's voice rang with disbelief.

"Cheryl and I prayed long and hard before we invited your family to move in," Levi explained. "We believe that *Gott* has brought you to us for a purpose and, if you will allow us, we would like very much to help if we can."

Tears settled in Wilma's eyes, but she nodded.

"That's wonderful, Levi," Kyle said, a tremor in his voice that touched Cheryl's heart. "We can't thank you enough."

He rose to shake Levi's hand and would have shaken Cheryl's as well, but lights flashing through the window on the front door stopped him. He glanced over his shoulder at Wilma.

"There's the coach with Blake. I should go and talk to him."

He moved toward the door, but Wilma snagged his arm before he reached it. "Kyle, please."

"It'll be fine, Wilma." He nodded toward Cheryl and Levi, his eyes hard despite his words. "We've got our friends to help us, right?"

He dropped his gaze to Wilma's hand. She immediately let it fall.

"Good. Now, what do you say we go and have a talk with our son?"

Wilma stood. Crossing to Cheryl, she murmured a quiet thank-you for dinner, but something about the way she looked at her chilled the blood in Cheryl's veins. Somehow, it was sad and frightened and angry all at the same time.

Cheryl clasped her hand. "You're welcome, Wilma. We'll talk again soon, okay? And in the meantime, let us know if there's anything we can do."

"I will. Thanks again," Wilma said, trailing Kyle to the door. The next moment, it clicked shut and closed her from view.

Chapter Fifteen

Cheryl rose early the next morning, her eyes tired and red from a night spent tossing and turning when she should have been sleeping. Slipping quietly out of the bed, she padded to the kitchen and put on a pot of coffee. A few minutes later, Levi joined her. Cheryl handed him a cup.

"Coffee will be ready in about two minutes."

He grunted and sank heavily into a chair at the table, then ran his fingers wearily through his hair. "Goot. I will need it today."

"You couldn't sleep either?"

He shook his head and rubbed his eyes, his lips stretched in a yawn. "I just kept thinking about Blake and what Kyle said about his coaches back home. Do you think this is true? Do coaches really make excuses to keep their players out of trouble?"

"Worse than that. From what I understand, it's not uncommon for some coaches to make sure their players get passing grades."

Levi's eyes rounded incredulously. "But, how can that be if they do not pass their tests?"

The pot finished brewing with a hiss and a cloud of aromatic steam. Cheryl carried it to the table to fill Levi's cup. "The lady I spoke to at the high school said some schools place a lot of importance on their sports," she said sadly. "More than on their students."

Levi sighed and shifted around to rest both arms on the table. "Well, at least Kyle and Wilma are doing what they can to help their son."

Cheryl poured herself a cup and sat down at the table next to Levi.

He watched her silently for a moment, then leaned forward to wrap his fingers around his cup. "What?"

She peered at him innocently. He lifted his eyebrows, waiting.

"It's just that…" She sighed and ran her finger along the rim of her cup. "Well, I had sort of an uneasy feeling watching Kyle and Wilma last night. I almost felt like they weren't telling us everything."

His chair creaked as he pushed from the table to lean against the back. "That is to be expected, ain't so? I am sure that sharing their son's problems with us must have been difficult."

"Hmm. Maybe." Cheryl took a sip of her coffee then fixed her gaze to the sky brightening outside the kitchen window.

"You think there is something else?" He smiled at her, as patient and loving as ever, understanding her ways.

She set down her cup. "The drugs I found in the store. I'm not sure they were Blake's. I can't even tell you why. Just a feeling."

"Perhaps you should ask him."

There was no doubt or reproach in his words, just trust for her instincts. And unwavering support. Oh, how she loved this man!

Cheryl reached out her hand, and Levi covered it with his own.

"I'll do that. Maybe later today. First, I was thinking I would pop in to talk to Wilma about what the coach said to them last night after they left here."

He nodded. "I am curious as well."

"Okay. I'll see what I can find out." Cheryl rose to take the eggs from the refrigerator. "Want me to make you an omelet while you get cleaned up?"

Levi glanced at the clock above the sink and nodded. "If you would not mind. That would be nice."

In response, she shooed him toward the bedroom while she pulled a frying pan from the cupboard. She had never been a very good cook, but Levi worked hard and learning to master a few things in the kitchen was one of the ways she showed him she appreciated him. Once the omelet was frying, she slid a couple of slices of bread into the toaster to go with it then set about emptying the sink of dirty dishes.

A short time later, Levi returned and gobbled down his breakfast, Rebecca woke and immediately cried to be fed, and just like that, Cheryl's day began in very short order. Before she knew it, the clock in the kitchen read ten.

She slid some shoes onto Rebecca's feet and then balanced the baby on her hip while she let them out the back door. By now, the sun was fully up and the climbing temperatures hinted at another warm day. Spotting wildflowers, Rebecca clamored to be let down, but Cheryl shushed her with a toy and then lifted her hand to the dawdy haus door. It flew open before she could knock and Blake stood staring at her, his eyes wide.

"Oh. I'm sorry." Cheryl stepped aside for him but instead of pushing past her, he moved back and held the door.

"Sorry about that. I didn't see you. Come on in."

"Thank you, Blake."

He nodded and twisted his head back to holler over his shoulder. "Mom, Mrs. Cheryl is here to see you."

His gaze dropped to Rebecca and he smiled. "Hey, little one."

He played with her a moment, and then finally, his eyes lifted to meet Cheryl's for a brief second. Just as quickly, he looked away, a flush creeping over his skin. "I suppose my parents told you what happened?"

"They kinda had to. You gave the coach my phone number," she reminded him gently. She hitched Rebecca higher on her hip. "Blake, are you all right?"

"Better than anything my father told you," he snapped, then dropped his head. "Sorry. Not your fault." He shuffled his feet and motioned toward the door. "I've gotta go. A friend offered to pick me up and take me to two-a-days."

Memories of her conversation with Mrs. Spalding flitted through Cheryl's mind. "The coach is letting you play?"

Instantly, she wished she could suck the words back in. Hurt shone on Blake's face, but something else too, something closer to anger.

"The coach didn't find any drugs in my bag. He said he can't do anything as long as I'm not caught in possession, but he's keeping an eye on me. Anyway, I can play for now so..." He motioned toward the door, and Cheryl moved to let him by. "I should be going. My ride'll be here any minute."

As though summoned, a car appeared in the driveway. It was an older model, like the type kids used to drive when Cheryl was in school. But judging by the mustache and goatee, the driver was much too old to be a student. Cheryl watched Blake climb inside, and then the car pulled slowly away.

"Cheryl?" Wilma stepped out from the kitchen, drying her hands on a towel. "I'm so sorry to keep you waiting." She looked past Cheryl out the door. "Is Blake gone?"

Cheryl nodded and clutched Rebecca's little hand. "He just left with his ride. Who, uh, who was that?"

"Oh, just an old friend from Wellington." She motioned back toward the kitchen. "Would you like some coffee? I just put another pot on to brew."

"Yeah, sure. That sounds good."

Cheryl cast one last glance at the taillights fading in the distance, then followed Wilma back to the kitchen. She set Rebecca on the floor to play. "I just thought I'd come by to check on you. How did it go last night?"

Wilma grimaced as she took two cups from the cupboard. "Things have never been easy between Kyle and Blake. It's gotten worse as he's grown older."

She held up a plastic bottle of powdered creamer. "Would you like some?"

"That'll be fine."

Though Wilma tried to appear calm, Cheryl noticed her hands shook as she set the creamer down next to a small bowl of sugar.

"Let me get you a spoon." She returned to one of the drawers and took out a plastic spoon wrapped in a plastic bag. She handed it to Cheryl with a wry grin. "Sorry. It's all I have right now. I'm going into town after Kyle gets his first check to pick up a few supplies."

"This is fine." She unscrewed the lid on the creamer and shook a little into her cup. "So, Blake said the coach agreed to let him play."

Wilma sucked in a breath, the movement so sharp, she splashed a bit of coffee out of her cup and onto her hand.

"Oh, here, let me help you." Cheryl handed her a napkin then grabbed a second one to mop up the spill. Wilma thanked her but failed to meet Cheryl's gaze as she did so.

Finally, Wilma balled up the damp napkin and threw it in the trash. "Sorry. It's just that football is so important to Blake. It's all he has, which is why I was so upset last night."

"I understand," Cheryl said quietly. "Have you thought about getting him some help?"

Wilma took a quick sip from her coffee cup, but Cheryl got the impression it was to mask the pained expression that twisted her features.

"Sorry. It's none of my business," Cheryl said gently, dropping her gaze to the brown liquid swirling in her cup.

Wilma set her own cup aside with a shake of her head. "No, it's fine. I'm doing what I can for him, but like I said before, things aren't easy between him and his father." She clasped her hands on the table and peered earnestly at Cheryl. "Look, I know it's probably hard for you to believe, but the drugs the boy saw in Blake's bag weren't his. He doesn't do drugs. He hates them, won't go anywhere near them in fact."

Cheryl watched her earnestly. "Then...whose drugs were they?"

She didn't respond right away but sat twisting the gold band on her ring finger around and around. "Sometimes," she said firmly, lifting her chin a notch, "people are left with no choice but the lesser of two evils."

"I'm not sure I understand," Cheryl said.

Wilma appeared to struggle a moment, then gave up with a shake of her head. "Blake's had to make a lot of tough choices in his life. I just don't want you to think that he's a bad kid, okay? He's got a good heart, even if it's not always obvious to people who don't really know him."

Unsure she understood what Wilma meant, Cheryl took a sip of her coffee and watched Rebecca play with her blocks.

"So, I'm heading into town in just a little bit," Cheryl said finally, when the silence between them had stretched thin. "Would you like to come? Since Kyle has the truck, I'd be glad to run you by the grocery store. And if you could use some money to tide you over, I'll be happy to loan you whatever you need."

"Oh, that's very nice of you, but I don't think so." Wilma motioned nervously around the house. "There are still so many things I need to finish up here."

Cheryl nodded and bent to pick up Rebecca. "All right, well I'll be gone a couple of hours. Just call if you need me to pick something up, okay?"

Seeing Wilma hesitate, Cheryl resisted the urge to smack her forehead. "Oops. I'm sorry. I forgot about you not having a phone."

But Blake had one. Once again, Cheryl wondered who was footing the bill. It was obvious his parents couldn't afford it, so if he wasn't selling drugs, where was the money coming from?

Cheryl cleared her throat carefully. "Um, Wilma? About Blake's phone—"

Wilma cut in, as though she'd read her thoughts. "His grandfather gave it to him. Paid the contract for a year."

"I see." She dropped her gaze to the floral tablecloth. Did she? They hadn't mentioned his grandfather before.

Wilma pushed up from the table. "I think we have everything we need right now. But thanks anyway."

Whining softly, Rebecca laid her head on Cheryl's shoulder.

"Okay, well I'd better go. This one is getting tired. Hopefully she'll nap in the car."

Cheryl ducked out with a wave, only stopping at the main house long enough to get Rebecca's diaper bag and refill her snack cup. By the time she got to town, Rebecca was indeed sound asleep, and Cheryl packed her into her stroller before heading into the grocery store for cereal and a few other staples. When she got to the checkout, she found that one of the teens from their youth group, Heather, was working. The store employed a lot of high school students during the summer and on nights and weekends during the school year. Cheryl angled the stroller toward Heather's lane and began pulling groceries out of the bottom.

"Hello, Heather."

"Hi, Mrs. Cheryl," she said brightly. Realizing that Rebecca was asleep, Heather slapped her hand over her mouth. "Ooh, sorry. Did I wake her?"

"No worries. She's a very sound sleeper," Cheryl said with a laugh.

She set a large box of cereal on the belt and then paused, remembering the conversation she'd heard between Heather and some of the other kids at church Wednesday night.

"Say, Heather, do you remember that guy you saw at football practice the other day? The one you said was a friend of Blake's?"

Heather's hand hovered over the cereal box. "Oh, you mean Steven?"

"Yes, him. Would you mind telling me what he looks like?"

A smile broke out on her lips. "He's a real cutie. He looks like a young Robert Downey, Jr. or something."

"Yeah?"

She nodded. "Uh-huh. He had one of those goatees." She rubbed her hand over her chin. A mechanical beep sounded as she ran the cereal over the scanner. "Anyway, I'm not a huge fan of facial hair, but it looks good on him. Some guys are like that, ya know? All rugged and stuff."

She gave a drawn-out sigh that made Cheryl want to roll her eyes. Or snap her fingers. Anything to make Heather focus.

She cleared her throat gently. "Uh, okay. What else can you remember?"

Heather rested her arm on the cash register, her nails clicking loudly against the side. "Well, let's see. He was tall, like a couple of inches taller than Blake. I do remember that. And he had sandy-brown hair." Cheryl nodded as Heather talked. Certainly, the man she had seen taking Blake to practice today fit his description. So, if he was Steven, what was he doing in town? She narrowed her eyes as she mulled the possibilities.

Heather finished ringing up her purchases then turned to her with a smile. "That'll be twenty-five dollars and thirty-nine cents. Anything else I can do for you?"

"Nope. That'll be all." Cheryl handed her the money then took the change. "Thank you, Heather. See you later."

She grabbed the bags of groceries and hung them over the handle of the stroller before heading out to her car to load everything in the trunk. Rebecca was still asleep, but she wouldn't be for much longer. Cheryl figured she might just have enough time to swing by the football practice field before making a pit stop for lunch.

A familiar car took up one of the parking spots as Cheryl neared the school—the same make and model as the one Blake's friend had been driving. It backed around as she pulled in. He was leaving?

Squinting as the car drove past, Cheryl caught a glimpse of the driver. He had sandy-brown hair and a goatee, just as Heather had described.

Steven, again. He and Blake left the house over almost two hours ago. Why was he just now leaving the school? She gritted her teeth. Wasn't that what drug dealers did—prowled around schools and restaurants where kids were known to hang out?

What if the ride to practice was just an excuse to get Steven close enough to make contact with other kids? Blake could be helping him!

Cheryl gripped the steering wheel tightly as she navigated the parking lot next to the football field. Practice was still in full swing and by the looks of things, the coaches wouldn't be cutting the players loose any time soon. That meant she'd have plenty of time to take Rebecca home and get back in time to ask Blake some questions.

She scanned the field. At wide receiver, Blake was easy to spot. Zach took longer to find, but Cheryl soon picked him out. So, they were both where they were supposed to be. Now, if she could just get back before either of them disappeared.

As she'd hoped, Naomi was only too happy to babysit for a couple of hours, especially after Cheryl explained why she needed a sitter. She warned Cheryl to be careful as she walked back to her car, then carried a wriggling Rebecca into the house.

While she drove back to the school, Cheryl wrestled with her thoughts. Was she right in asking Blake about Steven? What if she was wrong about him? And wasn't she just presuming that Blake was guilty when instead, she should be giving him the benefit of the doubt? Yet, it would be impossible to know without talking to him.

Her mind made up, Cheryl pulled into the parking lot to wait for practice to be over. She glanced at her watch several times as the minutes dragged by. Finally, around twelve thirty, a few of the players jogged off the field and headed toward the parking lot. Blake, she noticed, stayed behind to pick up shoulder pads and equipment. When he was done, he headed for the field house. He was the last to emerge, and stood looking out over the near empty parking lot.

Cheryl exited the car and held up her hand. Blake jogged over to her.

"Hey, Mrs. Cheryl. What are you doing here?"

"I just stopped by to talk with you, but it looks like maybe you need a ride."

Blake's mouth lifted in a crooked grin as he swung his bag over his shoulder. "Nah. My friend's just running a little late. What do you need to talk to me about?" Suddenly the grin disappeared, and his gaze sharpened as he leaned in toward the car. "Is everything all right out at the farm?"

His concern surprised her, not because he was worried for his family, but by the intensity of it.

She held up her hand. "Everything's fine, but since your ride's not here…" She motioned toward the empty parking lot. "Mind if we talk while you wait?"

He glanced into the back seat, and Cheryl shook her head. "Levi's mom is babysitting for me."

"Oh. Okay." He dropped his bag to the pavement with a thud and leaned back to rest against the hood. "So, what's up?" His tone took on a hard edge. "Is this about the other night?"

"In a way, I suppose it is. Still want to talk?"

She waited to see if he would clam up. Instead, he ducked his head and shrugged. "I guess so. I mean, I figured you would have questions."

"I do. A lot of them."

"The drugs weren't mine, if that's what you want to know."

"Which drugs?"

Blake lifted his head slowly, and his hand drifted toward his bag.

"I was talking about the drugs I found in the store, but now that you mention it..." She tipped her head toward his bag.

"Those weren't mine either," he muttered.

"So then how did they get there?"

He gave another noncommittal shrug.

"Okay." Cheryl crossed one arm over the other. "So, the friend who's picking you up. Is that Steven?"

He eyed her curiously. Cheryl motioned to his coat pocket. "I saw a text from him when you dropped your phone."

"Oh. Right." He nodded. "Yeah, that's Steven."

"Where is he from? Wellington?"

The turn in the conversation obviously made Blake nervous. He shuffled his feet and finally pushed away from the car and began pacing.

"Steven is...he's just a friend. He doesn't have anything to do with the drugs, I promise."

"Blake—"

His agitation growing, Blake swiped his hand through the air, then spun toward Cheryl so quickly she drew back a step.

"Mrs. Cheryl, please don't go around asking a bunch of questions. I know you mean well, and you probably think you're trying to help, but people who ask questions usually end up getting hurt."

Cheryl froze, not sure she'd heard right. "Wh-what did you just say?"

"You'll just be poking your nose where it doesn't belong," he continued, his voice rising.

He turned his head and looked right then left. Who was he looking for? He skidded to a stop and thrust out his hand, his finger aimed straight at Cheryl's face.

"And don't forget, you have Rebecca to think about."

She stiffened. The inside of her chest felt tight, as though her heart had stopped and her lungs weren't working. "What are you saying, Blake?" she asked, her voice low.

"I'm saying I don't want anything to happen to her. I'm saying the best thing you can do for her and for the rest of your family is to not get involved. I'm saying—"

He threw his hands above his head, misery lending a glassy sheen to his hazel eyes. "I'm sorry, Mrs. Cheryl. I really am. I wish we'd never come here."

Tires rumbled across the pavement, and the same car Cheryl had seen that morning pulled into the parking lot.

"There's my ride. I gotta go."

"Blake, wait," she called.

He shook his head and reached for his bag. "Sorry, Mrs. Cheryl. I'll see you later."

Calling him back would do no good. He'd said all he would, at least for now. Cheryl watched him go, his shoulders stooped and his tennis shoes making a scuffling sound on the pavement. When he reached the car, the man—Steven—ducked his head to peer at her through the window. Cheryl expected him to be angry...or threatening. He was neither. He met her gaze and gave her a tip of his head, then reached across the passenger seat to push open the door for Blake.

A minute later, they drove away.

Chapter Sixteen

Sweat dampened the palms of Cheryl's hands as she drove back to the farm. Thinking over Blake's words should have made her angry, or at the very least frightened, but she couldn't help feeling as though he'd meant them as a warning, spoken because he cared about her and her family.

"Mrs. Cheryl, please don't go around asking a bunch of questions. I know you mean well, and you probably think you're trying to help, but people who ask questions usually end up getting hurt."

It was the "please" that she couldn't get out of her head. The way it had sounded. The way he had looked at her when he said it.

"What is going on?" Cheryl wiped a tear from her eye and then smacked the steering wheel in exasperation. "Okay, Blake. If you won't tell me, I know who will."

She focused on driving the rest of the way home. When she arrived, she made a beeline for the dawdy haus. Steven's car wasn't there. Had he already dropped Blake off?

She raised her hand and knocked, shuffling impatiently from foot to foot while she waited for Wilma to answer. Finally the door swung open.

"Cheryl, what—?"

"Wilma, we need to talk," she said, probably more firmly than she needed to. But prodded by concern for her family, she met Wilma's gaze steadily. "It's important."

Wilma blinked and stepped back from the door. "All right. Come in."

"Thank you." Cheryl rubbed her hands together and entered the house. Behind her, Wilma closed the door with a soft click. The living room was quiet except for the sound of the television droning in the corner. She turned to look at Wilma. "Is Blake home?"

"Not yet." Wilma glanced at a clock on the wall. "But I expect him any minute."

"Good." Cheryl motioned toward the couch. "Can we sit? There's something I need to talk to you about."

"Of course." Wilma led the way, her hand smoothing and re-smoothing the hem of her T-shirt. She motioned Cheryl toward the couch and perched on a chair next to it. "So...uh...what..."

"I went by the school today to ask Blake about the drugs I found in my store," Cheryl said. Figuring blunt was best, she clasped her hands in her lap and explained as briefly as she could what Blake had said.

"He didn't mean it like it sounded," Wilma said. Her lips quivered as she ran her tongue over them. She sat forward, her hands clutching the arms of her chair. "I mean, I know he could have chosen his words better, but he was just worried, is all. Blake is a sweet boy. Very tenderhearted. And he just...he never wants to see anyone hurt."

"What is he worried about, Wilma? Or should I say, who?"

The seconds it took for her to answer stretched on. Finally, Cheryl shook her head.

"Okay. I'm really sorry, Wilma. I hate to do this but—"

Wilma's eyes took on a wild look. "Please. Please don't throw us out. I realize I'm asking a lot, but—"

She broke off, her mouth opening and closing with words she couldn't make herself say.

Cheryl shook her head reluctantly. "Look, I'm really sorry. I know things have been hard for you, but you have to understand, I must think of my family."

Thinking of the fear that had shot through her when Blake said Rebecca's name stiffened Cheryl's resolve. She lifted her chin and met Wilma's gaze calmly.

"Rebecca is just a baby. I'll do whatever I must to protect her."

"Of course you will. You're her mother. But I'm Blake's mother. I know he would never hurt anyone. If anything, he was trying to protect you. *And* Rebecca."

"Wilma—"

"We don't have anywhere else to go." Her voice grew louder and more desperate, her gaze more piercing. "If it will help, I'll talk to Blake. I swear I will. I'll tell him he has report to me every evening. I'll even let you check through his things."

"Wilma, I couldn't do that."

She grasped Cheryl's hand and held on tight. "Then whatever you suggest, we'll do it. Only please don't make us leave. This is the first time in almost a year that I really feel like Blake has a chance.

I know being here with your husband and Seth will be good for him. Please, just tell me you'll think about it."

By now, tears were running unchecked down Wilma's face, and Cheryl couldn't help but feel sorry for her. She rummaged in her purse, dug out a wrinkled napkin, and pressed it into Wilma's hand.

"Okay, Wilma."

She sniffed and blew her nose. "Okay?"

"I'll talk it over with Levi, and I promise we'll think about it."

Wilma's eyes brightened, and she nearly dove toward Cheryl to wrap her in a hug. "Thank you, thank you...oh..."

She drew back, and worry darkened her eyes again. "Cheryl, I have to ask you one more favor."

Sugar and grits. What was she getting herself into? She nodded hesitantly.

Wilma tore at the frayed edges of the napkin. "Please don't say anything to Kyle about this. If he knows we talked, he'll kick Blake out, I know he will."

"Kick him out....of the house?" The notion was so harsh, Cheryl shivered, and then lifted her hands in bewilderment. "But surely he wouldn't do that without making sure he had somewhere to go?"

"You don't know my husband," Wilma said, rising to pace. "He and Blake have fought before, and I don't just mean argue. The last time, they nearly came to blows. If it happens again, I know he'll send him away."

A tremor shook her shoulders, melting Cheryl's heart. She'd seen what strife could do to a family, first between her brother

Matt and her parents, and then Levi's sister Sarah. Though both rifts had now healed, it had taken years. She would spare Wilma that heartache if she could.

She stood and put her hand on Wilma's shoulder. "I'll let you decide how much to tell Kyle. In the meantime, I'm going to find a quiet place to pray while I wait for Levi to come home." She squeezed Wilma's hand. "We'll talk again soon, okay?"

Wilma nodded and followed her to the door. "Thanks again. I mean it. I'm so, so grateful."

Cheryl stepped out onto the porch, and Wilma waved goodbye with the tattered napkin. Realizing what she was doing, she drew it back and covered it with both hands.

Cheryl blew out a sigh and returned to the main house. She needed to pick up Rebecca, but before she did, she needed to talk to someone wiser than herself. Someone she could trust.

Mitzi.

Cheryl's computer sat atop the desk in the den. Hurrying over to it, she opened up Skype and put in Mitzi's contact information. It would be very early there...probably a couple of hours until the sun even rose over Papua, New Guinea, but maybe not too early since Aunt Mitzi often enjoyed doing her devotions before anyone else stirred.

While she waited for the call to connect, Cheryl sent up a silent prayer that her aunt would answer. She did, on the second ring. Her beloved face was a bit hazy, but her voice came in clear as a bell.

"Cheryl? Well, hello, darling. This is a pleasant surprise."

"Aunt Mitzi. Thank goodness I got you. I'm sorry for calling so early."

"It's quite all right, dear. Is everything okay back at the farm?"

Cheryl sank into a chair and dropped her chin to her palm. "Everything's fine, at least I think it is."

The screen flickered, and then Aunt Mitzi's picture sharpened so that Cheryl could read the worry in her gaze.

"What's going on, dear? What's happened?"

Cheryl quickly explained why she was calling then combed her fingers through her hair and let her hand fall to her lap. "I'm worried, Aunt Mitzi. I want to help Wilma, I really do, but I want to protect my family too. Especially now, with Rebecca in the house. Who knows what kind of people this could draw? Why, just today, I saw a strange man come by the house to pick up Blake. I should be worried about that, right?"

She cast her gaze toward the ceiling. "I don't know. Maybe it was a mistake taking strangers into the dawdy haus. We just never thought about the possibility of something like this happening. Do you think I should talk to Pastor Lory? And what about Seth and Naomi? I'm sure they're worried too." She sucked in a breath and then tapped the computer screen. "Well?"

Aunt Mitzi had been sitting so still while she listened, for a moment, Cheryl thought she'd lost the call.

Aunt Mitzi's lips lifted in a gentle smile. "Well, well...I hope you feel better now that you have all that out of your system."

"Well, I..." Cheryl turned her thoughts inward for a second, and then smiled. "Yeah, I suppose I do feel better."

"That's good. I'm glad." Aunt Mitzi's face grew larger as she leaned closer toward the camera. "Cheryl, sweetheart, why do you suppose this burden feels so heavy?"

She blinked in surprise. "That wasn't exactly the question I was expecting you to ask."

Aunt Mitzi laughed. "I know. But humor me."

Cheryl gave a slight shrug. "I don't know, I guess it's because I'm worried about Rebecca. And Levi too."

Aunt Mitzi shook her head. "I'm sure you are worried, but I don't think that's what is weighing on your spirit."

One thing Cheryl knew about her aunt Mitzi was that she always had a point, even if sometimes, it took her a while to make it. Cheryl forced herself to be still and wait.

"I think," Aunt Mitzi said slowly, "the reason the burden feels so heavy to you is because it was never yours to carry alone."

Cheryl let her shoulders sag. "I know. I need to trust God with this. But I have prayed about what I should do—"

"That's good, dear, and I wholeheartedly recommend that you keep it up, but that's not entirely what I meant."

Once again, Aunt Mitzi's words took her by surprise. Cheryl propped her elbows on the table, listening.

"Your husband, dear," she prompted gently. "God gave you a good, strong man with broad shoulders for a reason. Have you talked to him about what has been going on?"

"Of course! I mean, some of it, at least, I was planning to," Cheryl said, and then fell silent. In all honesty, she hadn't told Levi everything.

"Ah, there it is. Now you understand what I'm getting at."

"I didn't mean to leave him out, but you're right. I've been wondering and asking God what *I* should do instead of praying for my husband and asking what *we* should do."

"Mm...yes. That's good. Now don't get me wrong, dear. God gave you a brain for a reason, but when you go out on your own, without seeking counsel from the man God put beside you, it's like you're only using half your brain. You are two parts of a whole, after all."

Tears stung Cheryl's eyes as she nodded. "Guess I'm still getting used to that whole 'two shall become one' thing."

Aunt Mitzi chuckled. "Aww, don't be too hard on yourself. You lived on your own for a long time. It stands to reason that it will take a while before leaning on each other becomes second nature."

"Yeah, but after seeing how you and Uncle Ralph did it, or my parents and Levi's, I'd say it's worth the effort to learn."

"Most definitely," Aunt Mitzi said, smiling warmly.

They chatted a few more minutes before Cheryl said goodbye and signed off. It was early yet, only a quarter after two. Summertime meant long hours on the farm, and Levi would most likely be working until well after six. But maybe...

Cheryl grabbed her keys and headed outside. She still needed to pick up Rebecca, but maybe afterward she could make a pit stop, because now that she had a plan and focus, she couldn't wait to talk to Levi.

CHAPTER SEVENTEEN

R anger!" Rebecca pointed at the corral and then wiggled to be let down. Up until now, she had been riding quite happily on Cheryl's hip, but the moment she spotted the horse, she began flapping her hands and begging to run.

"Okay, we'll go see Ranger." Cheryl put her down then caught ahold of Rebecca's hand to keep her from running off. "But first, let's go see Daddy, okay?"

"Dada?" Rebecca's head swiveled back and forth as she looked for him.

"This way. Come on." Cheryl coaxed her with a gentle tug. "Oma said he's down by the barn."

"Dada!"

Her attention directed elsewhere, Rebecca took fast, tottering steps in the direction of the barn. Cheryl watched, riveted by the changes that had taken place in just over a year. Before long, she'd have to run just to keep up with her.

Rebecca continued to laugh and shout as they neared the barn. Levi emerged, a pleased grin on his face as he caught sight of them.

Rebecca threw out her arms and flew the last few steps, her chubby legs pumping as she jumped into her daddy's waiting embrace.

Levi covered her little face in kisses and then stretched out his free arm to wrap Cheryl in a hug. "This is a nice surprise. I was not expecting to see you until this evening."

"What is this? A little boppli has come to visit." Seth followed Levi from the barn, wiping his hands on an old rag.

"Opa!"

Having had enough of her father, Rebecca leaned over Levi's shoulder and stretched her hands to her grandfather. Seth laughed and plucked her from Levi's grasp.

"There she is ... Opa's girl. What have you been up to, little Rebecca?"

While Seth chatted with Rebecca, Levi dipped his head to look into Cheryl's eyes.

"Is everything okay at the house?"

She knew without asking that he meant the Dormans. She nodded. "Everything is fine, but we need to talk." She glanced at Seth. "Would it be all right if I snuck my husband away for a few minutes? I know you're busy, but ... "

Seth wagged his head at Rebecca playfully, making the baby giggle and pull on his beard. "Nonsense. We are not too busy for this little one, eh, my Rebecca?" He nodded to Levi and Cheryl, his tone more serious. "Take as much time as you need. Rebecca and I will go and check on Ranger."

"Thank you, Seth," Cheryl said, puffing out a sigh of relief.

Hoisting Rebecca onto his shoulders, Seth turned for the corral.

Cheryl glanced up at her husband. "I take it you told him what has been going on?"

Levi nodded and clasped her hand. "Ja, he knows. So, tell me what is bothering you that would not wait for this afternoon."

Cheryl shook her head and pointed out toward the barn. "Is Kyle in there?"

"Ja," Levi said, his brow crinkling. "Daed has him working on some of the harnesses and equipment for the petting zoo."

"Then let's go out to the pond so we can talk without being overheard."

An impish grin split Levi's lips, and he dipped his head toward hers. "Are you sure this is not just a ploy to get me out to your favorite spot?"

"No, but I'll keep it in mind for next time," she joked back.

Her husband always had a way of making her heart feel lighter, and today was no exception. She tucked her hand in his as he led the way toward the pond and the large rock that looked out over the water. The warm temperatures invited a chorus of buzzing insects, but this was truly one of Cheryl's favorite places on the farm so she swatted them away and climbed up onto the rock to sit.

"First, let me say that I'm very sorry for not telling you everything earlier," she said as Levi scrambled up to sit next to her.

His eyebrows rose, and he drew one leg up to rest his arm on his knee. "This sounds ominous. What haven't you told me?"

Beginning with her talk with Wilma, Cheryl explained everything that had happened, including her conversation with Blake on the way to football practice and everything in between.

"I know we said the Dormans being here was God's plan and purpose, but I'm worried, Levi. Especially after he brought up Rebecca."

She waited, searching his face for any sign of what he was thinking. Finally, she bumped her shoulder against his.

"So? What do you think?"

Levi lifted his head and looked out over the water, his gaze troubled. "In the flesh, I am frightened. I want to protect my family." He blew out a breath and fixed his gaze to Cheryl's. "But in the spirit...what has changed? We said bringing the Dormans here is God's plan. What part of that has changed?"

Cheryl looked down at her fingers splayed against the hard surface of the stone. "Nothing," she whispered.

"Cheryl."

She shook her head, her insides quaking. "Nothing has changed."

He slipped his finger under her chin, urging her gently to lift her eyes to his. "Then we will put our trust in Gott, ja? And we will continue seeking His will until we are certain of what He would have us do."

Slipping his arms around her waist, Levi tugged her close to his side, holding her until she felt a portion of peace creep back into her heart.

"I know you're right, Levi," she whispered against the warm fabric of his shirt. "It's just that, for the first time, I'm more worried for someone else's safety than my own. Rebecca is...it's like my heart is walking around outside of my body, and when I think of something happening to her, I can't help but feel panicked."

Levi pressed his lips to the top of her head. "And how do you think I felt all those months when you were rushing around solving mysteries? I was worried too, ain't so?"

Cheryl pushed upright and ran her finger under her nose. "Yes, but this is different. I'm an adult, and Rebecca is just a child."

Levi's eyes twinkled as he watched her.

She let out a laugh and then slapped his arm playfully. "All right, fine. I'm sorry I made you worry."

"You will always make me worry," he said with a smile, "because it is in your nature to want to help when there is a mystery to solve. But I would not try and change you, my Cheryl. I love you just as you are." He paused and tilted his head back. "But you should still be careful in your dealings with Blake, ain't so? We must not tempt Gott by acting foolishly or deliberately putting ourselves in harm's way."

Cheryl laid her palm against Levi's cheek. "You're right, and I would be a very thoughtless wife to do that after you told me how you've worried. I'll be careful, I promise."

He put out his hand to draw her near for a kiss. Her insides fluttering, Cheryl leaned toward her husband. For now and for always, she was content to let herself be drawn.

Chapter Eighteen

Beau's insistent meowing pushed Cheryl from the bed early the next morning. He looked out the window, then at her, then back out the window as though to signal that someone was at the door. Scrambling for a robe, Cheryl peeked over Beau's head to see who'd come calling. Elizabeth smiled brightly on the doorstep, a basket slung over her arm.

"Coming, Elizabeth," Cheryl called, and then hurried to open the door.

"Guder mariye, Cheryl." Elizabeth held out the basket and drew back the cloth that covered it. "Warm muffins from Maam. She said to tell you she's been thinking about you."

"Warm muffins?" Cheryl rubbed her eyes sleepily. "Elizabeth, what time is it?"

"Early, but Maam was up and baking before dawn and she wanted me to bring these over while they are fresh."

"Fresh, huh?" Cheryl leaned in and took a deep whiff, then widened her eyes at the pleasing aroma of vanilla and warm blueberries. "Okay, I'm awake. Come on in."

She held the door wide and followed Elizabeth to the kitchen. "Can you stay for a bit? I'll put on a pot of coffee."

Elizabeth smiled over her shoulder as she put the muffins on the counter, unbuttoned her sweater, and hung it on a hook next to the back door. "Stay? I am babysitting today, ain't so?" She held up the bag hanging from her shoulder. "I even brought my present for Grace to work on while I am here. I found the cutest pattern for a baby sweater."

Cheryl slapped her palm to her forehead. Saturdays were usually her day to check in at the Swiss Miss, but since she'd already been by a couple of times that week, she'd unconsciously scrubbed it from her mind.

"Sugar and grits, I forgot all about working at the store today. Oh, Elizabeth, I'm so glad you came by early."

Elizabeth leaned against the counter. "There's a reason I came by early. I've been wanting to ask you about something Esther said to me." She fiddled with a string on her prayer kapp. "I was at the singing last Sunday night and saw Esther leave with an Englisch boy. When I asked her who the boy was the next morning, she would not tell me. She just said that you know about him and that you understand her feelings because of your and Levi's courtship."

Cheryl's mind was whirling. How was she to answer Elizabeth truthfully and yet not come right out and tell her that her little sister was deceiving her? She reached for a muffin and broke it in half, stalling for a brief moment.

She took a deep breath. "It is true that I know about Esther seeing this boy. And while I understand that Esther wants to believe that her situation and Levi's are similar, I tried to tell her that because I was already a Christian when he and I became friends, and because we were not secretive, our courtship was very different."

Elizabeth sighed. "I did not think I was getting the whole story. I know that Esther feels it more keenly than I do that neither one of us are married or even courting. I do not wish for her to feel like she needs to 'settle' for anything less than God's best for her."

From her bedroom, Rebecca let out a small cry. Cheryl threw a panicked glance at the clock but Elizabeth gave a wave and set off down the hall.

"I will get her. Go ahead and get ready." She poked her head back into the kitchen with a mischievous grin. "Take your time. And thank you for being honest with me."

"You are welcome," Cheryl said, reaching for another muffin. She set the coffeepot on to brew, then carried the muffin with her to the bathroom to nibble on while she did her makeup.

In fact, with Elizabeth there to make Rebecca's breakfast, Cheryl had plenty of time to get ready and arrived at the Swiss Miss a full thirty minutes earlier than her usual time. She was glad to see that even at this early hour, patrons packed the store aisles. She smiled at several regular customers then ambled over to the front window where Ben and Rueben Vogel were engaged in their usual game of checkers.

"Good morning, gentlemen."

"Ah, Cheryl." Ben shot a glare at his brother and motioned her over with a vigorous wave. "You can be our mediator. What do you think? Is this a fair move, or is it cheating?"

Ben placed his finger on one of the red checkers and slid it sideways in a zigzag pattern.

Cheryl placed her finger to her lips. By the way he'd phrased the question, she figured red was Rueben's color. "Well, I'd have to say..."

"Yes?" Rueben leaned in close and slapped his brother's hand away from the checkers. "What do you think, Cheryl? It is a legal move, ain't so?"

"I think that both of you have been playing checkers a lot longer than I have," she said with a laugh.

Both men groaned good-naturedly, and then Ben craned his neck to look beyond Cheryl. "Where is your little one this morning?"

"Home with her aunt," Cheryl said. "And speaking of aunts, have either of you seen Esther this morning? The line at the checkout is starting to back up."

Both heads bobbed, and Ben pointed toward the back of the store. "She was cleaning over by the dry goods, eh, Rueben?"

He nodded and made to rise. "Ja, just so. Shall I fetch her for you?"

"No need," Cheryl said quickly. "I'm sure I can handle the counter while she's busy doing something else. Have fun, guys, and no cheating."

She wagged her finger at them and was rewarded with jolly laughter from them both. Pasting on a bright smile, Cheryl hurried to the counter and began checking out customers. Nearly twenty minutes later, the store had cleared out some, but Esther was still nowhere in sight.

Cheryl glanced at her watch. It was too early for her to be on her break. Lydia was working too, but even then, they always waited until the store wasn't busy before ducking out for a few minutes. She tidied up the area around the cash register and then set off in search of Esther. The dry goods aisle was empty, so either Rueben had been mistaken or Esther had moved off to do something else. Cheryl smiled at an elderly couple stooped over a stack of handmade textiles and continued looking.

Low voices carried from the area near the storage room. Tall stacks of boxes hid the speakers from view, so at first, Cheryl thought a couple of customers had inadvertently wandered near the back. Drawing closer, she quickly realized that it was Esther.

And she wasn't alone.

Cheryl bit off a groan. There had to be an explanation, and Esther deserved better than for her to jump to conclusions.

She cleared her throat before stepping around the nearest stack of boxes. "Esther, could I see you for a minute?"

Esther whirled toward her. In her hands was clutched a brown paper bag, the top rolled down several times. Zach stood opposite her, his mouth slightly agape. He ran his fingers through his hair at the sight of her. He looked guilty, all right.

Cheryl acknowledged him with a nod. "Hello again, Zach."

His gaze slid to Esther and back. "Uh, hi, Mrs. Miller." He maneuvered himself around them and headed toward the exit. "See you later, Esther."

He didn't look at Cheryl as she stepped aside to let him pass, and it was all she could do not to reach out and shake him.

Cheryl drew in a calming breath and blew it out through her nose. "Esther, what in the world—"

"It's not what it looks like," she said hastily. She started to put out her hand, realized she still held the bag, and quickly stuffed it behind her back. "Zach was just shopping."

Cheryl shook her head in disbelief. Surely she didn't expect her to believe that? "In the piles of inventory? What exactly did he hope to find?"

A blush darkened Esther's cheeks. "Well…we…didn't have any more Bible covers out front, so I came back here to look."

Cheryl folded her arms across her chest. "Zach wanted a Bible cover?" This time, she couldn't keep the skepticism from ringing in her voice.

Esther ducked her head. "I know how it sounds. His father's birthday is coming up." She eased toward the door, the bag still held securely behind her back. "He came by looking for a gift for him."

There was no point in arguing with her, but she couldn't help but feel disappointed. This was, after all, the second time she'd caught Esther alone with Zach. Cheryl motioned toward her hands. "Esther, what's in the bag?"

Esther hesitated a long moment, her cheeks slowly draining of color. Finally she pulled the bag out and held it in front of her. "This? It's nothing. Zach had an old jersey he wanted to give to a friend, but he didn't have time before practice. I told him he could leave it with me so his friend could pick it up here."

"Oh, okay. May I see it?"

Esther shied away from her outstretched hand with a frown. "It's nothing, Cheryl. Really."

"I know. You said that, but I'm still curious. May I?"

For several seconds, they stared at one another, both refusing to blink. Finally Esther dropped her gaze but kept her tight grip on the bag.

Cheryl lowered her hand, her heart—and her stomach—in turmoil. "Esther, what is going on with you? You've never acted like this before. I'm really worried about you."

"There is no need to worry," she said, lifting her chin. "I know you think Zach has turned my head, but that is not the case at all. I just want to help him."

"And you think this"—she motioned around the secluded corner—"is the best way to accomplish that? Esther, what if someone had seen you? Did you stop to consider what they might think?"

Esther gave a roll of her shoulders. "You're right, I should have been more careful, but Zach said he needed a favor and I didn't think it was a big deal. I mean, it's not like people couldn't see us. We were in plain sight the entire time."

"But Esther..."

A thousand reasons for avoiding even the appearance of impropriety flooded through Cheryl's brain. Before she could voice even one, Esther eased past her.

"I'm sorry, Cheryl. I will be more careful in the future. Now, I really should get back to work."

"Esther, wait." Cheryl held up her hand. "You asked me to help you prove the drugs we found here weren't Zach's, remember?"

She nodded warily.

"Do you also remember what you said?" Cheryl propped her hands on her hips. "You said you would do anything I asked, anything you could to help. But to be honest, I feel like you've been anything but helpful." She swallowed a sudden knot of hurt. "And you haven't been forthcoming with me."

Tears flooded Esther's eyes, and her shoulders drooped. "You're right." Her hand rose to her cheek, and she dropped her gaze. "I'm sorry, Cheryl. I wasn't trying to hide anything from you. I'm just…I just feel so torn."

She whirled to pace.

"Esther, watch out!"

Cheryl stuck out her hand in warning. With her head lowered, Esther couldn't see Henry as he rounded the corner. She ran smack into him and likely would have fallen had he not put out his arms to catch her.

"Oof!"

"Whoa. Esther, I am so sorry. I did not see you there."

"Oh, Henry." Her hand fluttered up to her prayer kapp, which had been knocked slightly askew. She righted it on her head and then smoothed the strings in place. "It was not your fault. I was in a hurry."

Realizing she had dropped the bag, Esther turned in a circle looking for it.

Henry spotted what she was looking for by his foot and bent to pick it up for her. "Here you go. You dropped this."

Esther took the bag, which had come unrolled in the scuffle, glanced inside, and then pressed it to her chest. Her gaze bounced from Cheryl to Henry. "Thank you," she said lamely.

"Is everything all right, Esther?" Concern colored Henry's voice as he leaned toward her. "Your face is white."

"He's right. You do look a little pale," Cheryl echoed.

"I'm fine." She grabbed the edge of her apron, pulling it straight with a jerk. "I just wish everyone would stop hovering, is all."

Henry fell silent at that, but her words only served to incite Cheryl's curiosity.

"You know, Esther, I've learned in my time here that it's usually only people who have something to hide who get angry when people who care about them ask how they're doing."

Esther said nothing but she did not meet Cheryl's gaze, which was odd, since she'd been about to open up *before* she looked inside the bag.

Cheryl stepped forward and put out her hand. "Esther, as your boss, I'm going to have to ask you to turn over that bag."

The words tasted bitter on Cheryl's tongue. She didn't want to take this approach, but with Esther not willing to answer her questions, what else was she to do? She held out her hand steadily, waiting. At first, she thought Esther might refuse. It was only after a long moment that she finally handed it over, the rustling of the paper loud in the quiet that had fallen around them.

Dread filled Cheryl's stomach. Zach had given Esther this bag. She knew it without a doubt. But did she really want to know what was inside? Her gaze drifted to meet Henry's. He stared back, his eyes wide and solemn.

A moment later, Cheryl's worst fears were realized.

CHAPTER NINETEEN

Henry's face darkened with concern. "What is it? What's in there?"

Ignoring him, Cheryl threw her hands up in frustration and disbelief, the bag rustling wildly. "Esther, this was so irresponsible. How could you take a bag from someone without knowing what was inside?"

"I *did* know! At least, I thought I did. And it wasn't just *some* person," she protested, her voice rising to match Cheryl's. "It was Zach. He told me just to hang on to it and that someone would be stopping by to pick it up."

"And you believed him without looking to see what it was?" Cheryl insisted.

A bit of the steel seeped from Esther's spine as she realized her mistake. She grabbed hold of the hem of her apron and began tugging at the edge. "He asked me not to," she whispered. "Zach is"—she glanced sidelong at Henry—"a friend. I thought I could trust him. I thought it would be okay."

Cheryl's blood pressure rose, and with it her temper. A still, small voice inside warned her to stay calm. She refused to heed it and shook the bag in Esther's face.

"But it's not okay, Esther. Do you realize how many people pass through here every day?"

"Of course I do," she said, a trifle indignantly. Her vim returning, she crossed her arms and poked out her chin. "I didn't do this on purpose. And I don't see how Zach's leaving something for me to watch is any of their business."

"Esther, this bag is full of drugs!" She jerked her thumb toward the exit. "That guy you claim is your friend? The one you thought you could trust? He *literally* just left you 'holding the bag.' What do you have to say about that?"

"What's this about drugs?"

All three of them froze as two familiar figures walked around the tall stacks of inventory.

"Chief Twitchell."

Realizing she'd said his name aloud, Cheryl swallowed a sudden knot of dread. Resisting the urge to hide the bag behind her back as Esther had done, she simply hugged it tightly to her stomach. "How nice to see you. And Officer Ortega. What can I do for you?"

"Too late, Cheryl," the chief said firmly. "I already heard what you said about the contents of that bag." Obviously in full official mode, he held out his hand. "May I see it, please?"

Her mouth dry, Cheryl handed over the bag and then took an instinctive step backward.

"It's…I…" No other words came. She watched silently as Chief Twitchell removed one of the small Ziploc bags, examined it, then dropped it back inside.

His gaze fell on each of them in turn. "Who does this bag belong to?"

Cheryl licked her lips. "Chief, I think I can explain—"

Esther stepped forward, her arms clasped around her middle. "It is mine...or...what I mean is...I was holding it for someone."

The chief's dark eyebrows rose and disappeared under the brim of his hat. "I've seen you in here before. Aren't you one of the Miller girls?"

She dropped her gaze to her plain leather shoes. "Yes, sir. Seth and Naomi are my parents."

"Esther, right?" He looked at her, then at the bag, and then her again. "And you say this bag belongs to you?"

"She misspoke. She was just holding it, Chief," Cheryl began.

Chief Twitchell held up his hand before she could finish. "Well, young lady?"

Esther nodded miserably.

The chief straightened to his full height—a considerable distance which he made more imposing by staring down his large nose—and propped his hands on his hips. "Are you aware of what's inside?"

Esther's eye twitched, and she shuffled her feet nervously. "I wasn't before. I am now."

"I see." He lifted his hand and rubbed his fingers over his chin. "May I ask how you came to be in possession of the bag?"

Indecision tore across Esther's face, and her lips turned in a frown. Finally, she ducked her head and said nothing.

"Esther, he's a police officer. You have to answer him," Cheryl whispered, urgency making her words sharp.

"This isn't a game, young lady," the chief added. "If you aren't willin' to answer my questions here, then I'm afraid I'm goin' to have to take you down to the station."

She couldn't help it...a gasp escaped Cheryl's lips. Esther wasn't a child, but she'd lived a fairly sheltered life. If the chief was trying to scare her into a confession, surely he could handle it another way. She angled herself sideways, between him and Esther.

"Chief, surely that won't be necessary," she said, her voice low. "Perhaps we could talk in my office. I'm sure we could work all of this out there."

He pushed his hat back off his forehead, his finger scraping his scalp. "All right, Cheryl. Let's try it your way first." He turned to Officer Ortega. "Take Miss Miller into Cheryl's office and get her statement."

Cheryl watched in dismay as the police officer took Esther's arm and escorted her away from their group. "But, Chief Twitchell, she wasn't really in possession. I mean, technically she was, but the drugs don't belong to her."

"According to her, they did." He sighed and pressed his hand to her arm. "Drugs like this are becomin' a serious threat to our community, especially the last couple of weeks. You're a parent now too. I'm sure you can see why I want to nip the problem before it gets out of hand."

"Of course I do, Chief, but Esther isn't like..."

She paused. Esther had been doing a lot of things in recent days that weren't typical of her, but she wasn't a drug dealer. Cheryl swallowed hard. Ignoring Henry's wide eyes fastened on her, she pushed on.

"We've all made mistakes. Esther would never knowingly help someone deliver drugs."

Chief Twitchell gave a dissatisfied grunt. "Even so. Not tellin' me where those drugs came from is a failure to cooperate. She is hinderin' the investigation of an illegal substance." He shifted his lanky form and rubbed his fingers down his long nose. "Do you understand what that means?"

He couldn't put it more bluntly than that. Cheryl held her breath. Next to her, she sensed Henry doing the same.

"Yes, I understand, Chief Twitchell. I'm sure Esther will cooperate when she fully understands the gravity of her situation."

His head jerked. "Good. Now, we're gettin' somewhere."

"Chief Twitchell, Esther is not the person you want," Henry said.

Cheryl stared at him. Did he know the bag was Zach's?

The chief narrowed his eyes at Henry, his brow drawn in a perplexed line. Though he was much slimmer, Henry stood at an even height with him. He drew his shoulders back and locked gazes with the chief.

Henry glanced down at the bag in Chief Twitchell's hands. "That bag doesn't belong to Esther. It belongs to me. She was holding it for me."

Chapter Twenty

The frown lines deepened on Chief Twitchell's face. For a full second, he simply stared at Henry. Finally, he let his shoulders slump and shook his head.

"Henry, I've known your family almost as long as I've known my own. There's no way this bag belongs to you. Now, I have to tell you, if you're tryin' to protect someone, this isn't the way to do it."

Henry's chin lifted a notch. "You have it wrong, Chief. I am not protecting anyone. Esther did not know who the bag was for. That is the truth."

Exasperation made the chief's face pink. He puffed out a breath, his fingers tugging at his collar. "Henry, this is perjury. You do realize that. At the very least, you're impeding an investigation."

Cheryl's gaze bounced helplessly between the chief and Henry. He knew Henry was lying. They all knew it. Cheryl took a step forward and cleared her throat.

"Chief, the bag came from Zachary Waller. I was here when he gave it to Esther."

Chief Twitchell tucked the bag under his arm then took out a pad and pencil and jotted something down. "You witnessed this exchange?"

Cheryl bit her lip. "Well, to be honest, I didn't actually see him hand her the bag, but Esther did admit to me that he gave it to her to hold. He told her that someone would be coming by to pick it up. He didn't tell her who," she added quickly.

"It was me. I was the one he said would be coming by," Henry said. "Esther was just caught in the middle. She knew nothing about any of this. In fact, I told Zach to give it to Esther because I knew she would not look inside if he asked her not to."

"Henry, you're making this worse," Cheryl chided. "And you're not helping Esther by lying."

Chief Twitchell, however, didn't seem convinced. He angled his chin toward Henry, the tip of his pencil hovering over his pad of paper. "I assume Zachary Waller will corroborate your story?"

Henry set his jaw stubbornly. "I cannot speak for Zach."

A grunt rumbled from Chief Twitchell's throat. He jabbed the end of his pencil against the paper. "All right, then suppose you tell me where the drugs came from?"

"Chief, you don't really believe that Henry was the person picking up that bag?" Cheryl said.

"According to Henry, he is," he said firmly. "Well, Henry?"

"I don't know where they came from," he said, his face a stoic mask.

"What about after you picked them up? What did you intend to do with them?"

"Henry, don't answer that. Not until you've spoken to a lawyer," Cheryl said quietly.

"I don't need a lawyer," Henry said.

Cheryl crossed her arms. "At this point, I don't think you have any idea what you need, Henry."

He lifted his chin stubbornly. "Fine. I don't want one then."

Cheryl turned to Chief Twitchell. "Don't listen to him. He has no idea what he's getting himself into."

Henry dropped his gaze.

Chief Twitchell slid the pad and pencil back into his shirt pocket and then reached behind his back for his handcuffs. "She's right, Henry. You don't have to answer, but cooperating will certainly help your case. Are you sure you don't want to tell me anything else before we head down to the station?"

Cheryl looked on helplessly as Henry gave a stubborn shake of his head. Surely, this couldn't be happening. Tears formed in her eyes as Chief Twitchell snapped the handcuffs on Henry and read him his rights.

Cheryl watched in disbelief. This had to be an act. Surely Chief Twitchell was just trying to scare Henry into telling the truth. But how far would he let it go?

"Chief."

He shrugged and led Henry out from around the stacks of inventory. "I'm sorry to do this, Cheryl, but I'm afraid I'm going to have to take him in."

"But just for questioning, right? There's really no need to lead him out in handcuffs."

Chief Twitchell eyed her steadily. "I'm not bringing him in for questioning. As of this moment, I'm placing him under arrest."

Cheryl pressed her hands to her stomach, where a sick feeling was causing her to feel ill. "Henry, would you like me to call your parents?" she asked. It wasn't much, but it was the only thing she could think of that might help.

He blinked away the hurt welling in his eyes and shook his head. "Ne. Danki, Cheryl, but I would rather not involve them."

That said, he turned and let Chief Twitchell lead him away. Several people stopped to gawk as they walked past. Henry hung his head, and Cheryl knew he had to be feeling the weight of the shame brought on by their stares. If there was a blessing in any of this, it had to be that the store had cleared out some. She hated to think what would have happened had Chief Twitchell come in when it was packed with customers.

Hearing a soft sob, Cheryl turned to see Esther coming toward her following Officer Ortega, who nodded at Cheryl as she continued through the store and out the front door. Esther stood with both hands over her face and tears seeping through her fingers.

"Oh, Esther." Tucking her arm around her shoulders, Cheryl whispered, "Meet me in my office. Stay out of sight as much as you can. I'm going to flip the sign and close us up early."

Rubbing her hand under her nose, Esther nodded and whirled, her apron fluttering as she scurried away. Cheryl lifted her eyes to the ceiling and breathed a short, desperate prayer.

"God, give me wisdom. I have no idea what to do right now."

Curious murmurs floated throughout the store, or maybe it was only her imagination that made her scratch her tingling ears. Regardless, Cheryl couldn't check out the few stragglers wandering through the store quickly enough. She even ushered out Ben and Rueben with only an apology and no explanation. Finally, she taped a sign to the door and made her way to the office.

Esther sat bent over in one of the chairs, sobs shuddering through her frame. Her head jerked up at her entrance. "Oh, Cheryl, what are we going to do?"

"Do?" Cheryl paced the small confines of her office. "Esther, it should have already been done. You should have told Chief Twitchell the truth when he asked you." Seeing her stricken face, Cheryl sucked in a deep breath and continued more quietly. "All right, aside from the embarrassment that Henry just suffered, I don't think it's too late. We'll just drive down to the station and tell the chief the truth."

To her relief, Esther nodded in agreement and stood. "All right, but first—"

Cheryl stopped pacing to hold up her hand. "Whoa, there are no 'buts' here, Esther. The longer we delay, the worse things will be for Henry. We simply cannot let him be arrested for something he didn't do."

"Of course not. I agree with you."

Cheryl crossed her arms angrily. "And?"

"And I will go with you, but first..." She paused and rubbed her palms over her skirt nervously. "I need to call my parents and let them know what is happening. After that, we'll go down to the station and I will tell Chief Twitchell everything."

Much as she wanted to get moving, Cheryl knew Esther was right. Seth and Naomi needed to know what was going on. She motioned toward the phone on the desk. "Okay, but make it quick."

Esther shot a harried glance at the clock on the wall and then nodded. "I will. May I borrow your phone? I...I would like a moment to speak with my parents in private."

Cheryl slid it from her purse and placed it her hand.

She clasped it to her chest. "Thank you. I'll be right back."

Without waiting for Cheryl's response, she hurried across the office and threw open the door. Cheryl didn't need to ask where she was going. Deep down, she knew. She wasn't going to call her parents, at least, not just them. She was going to call Zach. Maybe she thought if she told him what had happened, she could convince him to come with them to the police station. Cheryl had her doubts. Zach didn't seem like the kind of stand-up guy who would own up to his mistakes.

Snatching the phone from her desk, Cheryl placed a call to Seth and Naomi and another to Levi, leaving messages both times, then paced the floor and counted the minutes until Esther returned.

In fact, it was a little over fifteen minutes before Cheryl heard the bell chime over the front door. She stepped out of her office and met Esther by the counter. Tear stains streaked her face, and her hair, normally so neat, hung from her prayer kapp in wisps.

Even though it was what she had expected, Cheryl couldn't help feeling sorry for her.

She rounded the counter and pulled her into a hug.

"Are you ready to go?" she whispered.

Esther squeezed her tightly and then nodded. "Ja, I'm ready. Let's go."

They completed the drive to the station in silence. It was only a couple of blocks, but Cheryl took her time getting there in hopes that by the time they arrived, Esther might have regained her composure. What thoughts might be going through her head, Cheryl had no idea. She kept her face to the window, and every now and then, lifted her hand to wipe another tear from her cheek.

Cheryl pulled up to the one-story brick building and parked. "We're here. Are you ready?"

Esther's fingers twisted on her lap, but she nodded. "I'm ready. I'm only sorry I didn't tell the truth in the first place."

"I am too." Cheryl laid her hand on Esther's arm. "What about Zach? Is he meeting us here? What did he have to say about all of this?"

Anger flashed in Esther's eyes and just as quickly faded. She didn't attempt to hide the fact that she'd called him. She simply pulled Cheryl's phone from her apron pocket and laid it on the dash. "He said he could not go to the police because an arrest could hurt his chances for a football scholarship. I asked him to at least tell me where the drugs came from but he wouldn't, no matter how much I begged. He even said it was better if Henry took the fall because the police would go easier on him because he is Amish."

Cheryl gritted her teeth, unable to keep her anger from showing even though she tried. "That skunk. What else did he say?"

"I told him I could not let Henry take the blame for something I did. I said I would tell the police so." She blinked rapidly against a sudden onslaught of fresh tears. "I thought this would push him to tell the truth, but he...he..." She drew a quivering breath and stared out the window. "He said he thought that might be best, because the police would be even more lenient with an Amish girl."

Cheryl's gasp ripped through the quiet car. She wanted to yell. She wanted to rant and rave at Esther and tell her that she'd tried to warn her. She wanted to hit something—namely Zach—and force him go to the police with the truth. But she could do none of those things. They wouldn't help.

Cheryl reached for her purse and pushed the strap over her shoulder. "Come on, Esther. Let's go inside."

Drawing in a shaky breath, Esther put her hand to the door handle. "Cheryl?" She hesitated and looked across the seat at her. "Will I be arrested?"

Cheryl licked her lips nervously. "To be honest, I don't know," she said, and wished she had a better answer to give her. "But like Chief Twitchell told Henry, it will help that you're cooperating. Just be sure you don't hold anything back this time, okay?"

The door handle clicked as Esther pulled it back and stepped out onto the sidewalk. She waited while Cheryl circled around the car then lifted her chin and thrust her shoulders back.

"Ja," she whispered, her gaze fixed on the path ahead. "No holding back. Let's go."

Chapter Twenty-One

The Sugarcreek Police Department was a modest place, set back from the main street that ran through town. Over the last few months, Cheryl had been inside it several times, but never for something like this. Anxiety wormed up from her stomach and made her wish Levi were next to her. He would know what to do, what to say, to make things all right. Obviously, he had yet to check his messages.

Next to her, Esther fidgeted on a blue vinyl chair, her fingers nervously plucking the end of her sleeve. Delores, the receptionist, had promised to return after she'd asked the chief for permission for them to see Henry, but that had been over fifteen minutes ago and there was still no sign of her.

Esther leaned forward, craning her neck to see past the counter to the hallway. "What is taking her so long?"

Even her whisper seemed loud in the quiet police station lobby.

"I'm not sure," Cheryl whispered back. "Maybe he's still giving his statement to the chief."

"Then shouldn't someone tell the chief we are here? We have information he needs."

Esther cut off when the frosted door bearing Chief Twitchell's name swung open. He stepped out with the receptionist on his heels.

"Delores, would you please let Henry know that he has visitors?"

"Yes, Chief." Behind her thick, black glasses, Delores shot an apologetic glance in Cheryl's direction.

Cheryl sighed. How much did she know? Delores disappeared through a door that led to the cells, and Cheryl's heart sank. Henry was behind bars?

She stood and walked to the counter. "Thank you for letting us see him, Chief."

He laid his large hand on the counter with a sigh. "Well, I hate having him in there, but until he changes his story, my hands are pretty much tied."

"I know. Hopefully we can do something about that after Esther's had a chance to talk to him."

Chief Twitchell shot a glance at Esther over Cheryl's shoulder. "Has she said anything to you yet?"

She nodded. "Unfortunately, she's had a rather painful reality check. I'm pretty sure you won't have any trouble getting anything she knows out of her now."

His head bobbed. "Good. That's good."

"Chief?" Cheryl leaned in toward the counter and lowered her voice. "How much trouble is Henry in? I know he said he didn't want to, but should he be contacting an attorney? And what about Esther?"

Sam Twitchell was a good man. Granted, they hadn't always seen eye to eye, but Cheryl knew she could trust him. If he advised her to start looking for an attorney, she'd be on the phone in a heartbeat.

He leaned both elbows on the counter. "As far as Esther is concerned, it's up to her. At this point, I just want to ask a few questions. If it gets to be anything more than that, I'll step back and give you time to make a phone call."

Cheryl blew out a sigh. "Thank you, Chief."

"Henry, on the other hand, is another matter," he continued. "A case could be made that he intended to sell the drugs, which would mean a much stiffer penalty if he's convicted. I asked him if he wanted to contact an attorney before he gave his statement, but he refused."

"Does he have any idea of the kind of trouble he's facing?"

"He claims he does. I'm hopin' a little time in a cell will convince him otherwise. Regardless, he's nineteen. The law considers him an adult. He can make his own decisions."

Cheryl shook her head and then the chief straightened off the counter and beckoned to Esther. "Miss Miller, if you'll follow me?"

Esther rose and swept her hands down the length of her apron. At the door, she paused and looked at Cheryl. "Will you come with me?"

The chief nodded his agreement, so Cheryl skirted the counter and joined her at the door. "Of course."

The chief looked at his watch and then sternly at Esther. "I'll give you ten minutes. After that, we'll talk in my office. All right?"

Esther looked at Cheryl, who nodded.

"Good. Officer Spencer will show you to Henry's cell. Be advised, he will have to remain present while you two talk. Do you understand?"

"Ja...I mean yes. Thank you."

Esther gave him one last nod before proceeding down the hall behind Officer Spencer. When they reached the end, Cheryl bit her lip, expecting to see Henry huddled on the bed, or at the very least hunched over in a chair. Instead, he stood by the window, the sun shining on his face, his eyes closed and his lips moving in silent prayer.

"Henry?"

Hearing Esther call his name, he opened his eyes and moved toward them. "Esther, what are you doing here?"

She rushed toward the cell but a gentle "Ahem," from Officer Spencer pulled her up short before she clutched the bars.

"I came to see you." Her face blanched, and she lowered her voice to a frightened whisper. "Henry, you should not be in here. This is all my fault."

Henry shot a glance at Officer Spencer then stepped forward to clutch the cell bars. "Ne, it is not your fault, Esther. The choice was mine. Do you understand? It was mine."

In fact, his meaning was quite clear, even to Cheryl. She moved to Esther's side. "Henry, we both understand what you're trying to do, but you really need to stop and think what all of this could mean. Chief Twitchell just told me that if it looks at all like you intended to sell those drugs, you could be in a lot of trouble."

Esther's eyes widened. "I have to tell him the truth. The drugs were from Zach. He is the only one who knows who the drugs were for, and who gave them to him. If the chief talks to him, he will confess."

Henry lowered his head, and his knuckles whitened against the bars. "Knowing Zach, he will deny knowing anything about the drugs. He will let the blame fall to you even if it means you could go to jail." He lifted his gaze to meet hers. "I will not let that happen."

"Henry." His name fell from her lips, a mixture of disbelief and awe making her voice weak.

Officer Spencer straightened attentively as Henry pressed himself to the bars but when he did not reach through, he relaxed against the wall.

"I will do whatever I must to protect you, Esther," he said, his voice breaking for the first time since they'd arrived. "Even if it means sitting in this jail cell."

Her head shook, and she whispered something in Pennsylvania Dutch. "I cannot let you do that," she continued. "It is not right. I will tell the chief that I knew what was in the bag when Zach gave it to me."

"He will just think you are trying to protect me."

"Ne," she said firmly. "Cheryl saw Zach give the bag to me. It is reasonable that I knew what was inside."

"She saw you with the bag, she did not see him give it to you," he said sadly, backing away from the bars. "And you have already told her *and* the chief that you did not know what was inside. Changing your story now would only make you look like a liar."

"Two minutes." Officer Spencer tapped his wristwatch then resumed his silent vigil against the wall.

Esther's frightened gaze leaped to Henry. As he backed away, she stepped closer. "You cannot do this. I will not let you." When he refused to look at her, the desperation grew in her voice. "It is a sin to tell a lie. Cheryl, tell him."

Cheryl put her hand to Esther's shoulder. "He knows that, Esther, but right now, all he's thinking about is you."

She shook off Cheryl's hand and clutched the bars, ignoring the warning look Officer Spencer directed her way. "Ne! Henry, listen to me, we will speak to Chief Twitchell together. Once he hears that you were just trying to protect me, he will understand why you said the bag was for you."

"Will you also tell him that Zach was using you to help him spread drugs in our town?"

The sadness in Henry's voice broke Cheryl's heart. She glanced at Esther, who stood frozen, her face a pale mask.

"Yes. I will tell him."

"Esther." Cheryl placed a light touch on her elbow. "We should go."

She shook her head and clung tighter to the bars. "I know what you are trying to do, Henry Detweiler, but I won't let you."

The door to the hall opened, and Delores poked her head inside and looked at Esther steadily. "Miss Miller, the chief is ready for you."

Esther continued to stare pleadingly at Henry, so Cheryl acknowledged Delores with a nod then turned back to the cell. "Esther, please."

Slowly, she backed toward the door, tears coursing her face. Giving one last look at Henry, she turned and dashed into the hall.

"Sorry, Cheryl," Delores said as they exchanged a glance.

"It's okay. I'll just be another minute."

Delores ducked out after Esther, and Cheryl looked over at Officer Spencer. She motioned toward the cell. "May I?"

He nodded, and she moved closer to grasp the cold iron bars. "Henry, I know what you're trying to do, but you have to realize, this is only going to make things worse."

"How?" He lifted his hands and let them fall dejectedly. "What could be worse than seeing Esther sitting here in this place?"

Cheryl cleared her throat. "Well, for one thing, you could be keeping the police from questioning Zach."

"Ne. They will bring him in to ask him where he got the bag, but he will say he did not know anything about it."

"How can you be sure?"

Henry gave a low grunt. "Because I know him." Hope flickered in his gaze. "What about the bag? Will they be able to tell it belonged to Zach if they find fingerprints on it?"

"I'm afraid not," Cheryl said sadly. "Lifting fingerprints from paper is very difficult. And even if there were prints, they would have been ruined when we kept handling the bag."

He dropped his head.

"Henry," she said after a moment, "if Zach thinks you're willing to be a scapegoat, he's just going to be that much more resolved to stay quiet. You have to tell the chief the truth—you had nothing to do with those drugs."

Once again, the door creaked open and Delores looked inside. "Henry, your parents are here to see you. Would you like to speak to them?"

Her words only added to the misery sagging his shoulders. He rubbed his palm over his face with a quiet groan. Finally he nodded.

"Ja, I will speak to them."

Cheryl glanced over her shoulder and back at Henry. "I'll step out and give you some time alone with them."

If he heard, he didn't show it. Her heart heavy, Cheryl walked out into the hall. The Detweilers passed her, Mr. Detweiler's face dark with worry and anger. Mrs. Detweiler shuffled along behind him, her face a mixture of disbelief and fear. Cheryl's heart went out to her. What must she be thinking right about now?

From the front of the station, Delores beckoned. Cheryl hurried toward her, her insides a twisted riot of emotions.

Studying Cheryl from behind her thick glasses, Delores pursed her lips and reached under the counter for a box of Kleenex.

"Here. You look like you could use one of these." She pushed the box toward Cheryl and then rested her elbows on the counter. "Everything all right? What is going on?"

Cheryl pulled a tissue from the box and used it to wipe the dampness from her cheeks. "One, everything is not all right, and two, I wish I knew." She balled up the used tissue and tossed it into the trashcan next to Delores's desk. "Is Esther in with the chief?"

Delores stuck the tip of her pencil in her mouth and nodded. "He looked none too happy about it though."

"Ugh. I bet. He'll be in a mood before I get a chance to speak with him. And I still have to talk to Esther's parents and fill them in on what's going on."

She checked her phone. No messages, but that didn't surprise her. Seth and Naomi did not keep a phone in the house. They used a phone shack with an answering machine, so it often took some time before they returned a call. And Levi was likely working in the field or in the barn so talking with him would have to wait. That meant the burden of doing what was best for Esther settled squarely on Cheryl's shoulders.

She shivered and paced across the room to the door and back. "Delores, have you ever met Henry's parents?"

Delores shoved the pencil behind her ear and shook her head. "They seemed really upset. His father was mumbling something about church discipline."

"What?"

Delores pushed her glasses higher onto her nose. "Doesn't that mean shunning or something like that?"

"Maybe." The fluttering in Cheryl's stomach grew. "What exactly did he say?"

"I couldn't hear it all," Delores admitted. She pointed toward the blue chairs. "He sat there muttering something about forcing him to repent or face church discipline."

"But he hasn't done anything wrong." Cheryl groaned and pushed her fingers through her hair. "Poor Henry. I bet his parents are furious with him right about now."

As though to punctuate her point, the door to the hall flew open and Mr. Detweiler strode out. He didn't look at Delores or Cheryl on his way to the front door, just kept his gaze fastened straight ahead. A few seconds later, he was followed by Mrs. Detweiler. She looked angry too, but her eyes were red as though she'd been crying, or fighting not to.

Spying Cheryl, she walked over and stood wringing her hands anxiously. "You are Esther Miller's sister-in-law, ain't so?"

Delores sucked in a breath and busied herself with stacking the papers on her desk.

Cheryl stepped away from the desk and invited Mrs. Detweiler to do the same with an outstretched hand. "Yes, I'm Cheryl Miller. Esther's brother Levi is my husband."

Mrs. Detweiler dipped her head in acknowledgement. "It is a pleasure to meet you."

Cheryl relaxed a bit. "You too. I wish it were under better circumstances."

She nodded. "This is bad, for sure and for certain." She motioned toward the cells. "My Henry is innocent, of this I am sure. He would never do drugs."

"I believe that," Cheryl said, and meant it.

"Danki." Mrs. Detweiler's face twisted with pain. "Henry is a goot boy. He cannot pay for a crime he has not committed."

"I agree," Cheryl said softly.

Her face brightened. "Then, you will help? You will speak to the Millers for us?"

Cheryl frowned in confusion. "The Millers? I don't understand."

Mrs. Detweiler's head bobbed rapidly. "Esther will submit to their authority. If they ask her to tell the police that Henry was not involved, she will listen."

"Esther is already doing that," Cheryl said quickly. "In fact, she's with the chief right now trying to explain what really happened. But Henry is adamant the bag of drugs was his. I'm not sure that anything Esther says at this point will make any difference."

Mrs. Detweiler pressed her lips together angrily. "Henry is a goot son. He has never disobeyed our wishes, not once, but he has loved Esther since they were kinder. I think he said the drugs were his to protect her, but he would not admit it, even when my husband threatened church discipline."

What could she say? She agreed with everything Mrs. Detweiler said. "I'm sorry," she said at last.

Mrs. Detweiler eyed her steadily for several long seconds, then shook her head sadly and followed her husband out the door.

Watching her go, Cheryl blew out a breath. "This is crazy. I have to do something." She glanced at Delores. "Do you by any chance still have my cell phone number?"

"Of course." She picked up her phone and wiggled it. "Right here."

Cheryl hooked her purse over her arm and headed for the door. "Good. Will you call me once Esther is finished with the chief? I have somewhere I need to go."

Delores frowned in confusion. "Sure, but where—?"

"Can't talk now, but I'll be back as soon as I can." Cheryl paused with her hand on the door handle. "And, Delores, whatever you do, don't let Esther leave, okay? Let her know I'll be back to pick her up so we can talk to her parents together."

"I'll do what I can," she said, glancing toward Chief Twitchell's office uncertainly.

"Thank you."

Cheryl hurried to her car, climbed inside, then grabbed her phone from the dash where Esther had laid it. Esther had used her phone to call Zach, so his should be the last number dialed. Swiping across the screen, she waited a split second for the home page to load then found the number in her recent calls. With anger making her fingers shake, she hit the dial button and pressed the phone to her ear. A deep, male voice answered on the second ring.

"Hello?"

Cheryl swallowed hard and forced her voice to remain calm. "Hello, Zach?"

"Uh, no, sorry. Who is this?"

"My name is Cheryl Miller. I'm a friend of Esther's. Could I speak to Zach, please?"

"Oh, hi, Mrs. Cheryl."

Cheryl paused as a spark of recognition dawned. "Sorry, who am I speaking to?"

There was a swishing noise in her ear, as though the person on the other end of the line were adjusting their phone, and then the voice returned.

"This is Blake, Mrs. Cheryl. Blake Dorman."

CHAPTER TWENTY-TWO

Blake? Cheryl pulled the phone from her ear, checked the number, then clenched it tightly and placed it back to her ear. "Blake. Hi. Um...where are you?"

"I'm at football practice, or I was. We just left."

"We?"

"Me and Steven. He's giving me a ride."

Steven again. Who was this man? Cheryl pushed the question aside and focused on the reason for her call. "Blake, did Esther call you a little bit ago?"

"Esther?"

He sounded genuinely confused. That, or he was a very good actor.

"Levi's younger sister. She works at the Swiss Miss."

"Oh. Um...no, I haven't talked to any of his sisters."

Cheryl frowned. She distinctly remembered Esther saying they'd met. He'd come into the store with some of his friends. So why was he acting like he had no idea who she was?

She sucked in a breath. Could it be she had it wrong? Could it be that Blake had given Esther the bag, and Zach was in the process of picking it up when she interrupted? She shook her head. No, it was still possible that Zach had given her the bag. But Blake could have been the intended recipient. She could have been calling him to warn him not to stop by the store to pick it up. Her stomach sank. Would Esther do that? Cheryl's first instinct was to say no, of course not, but could she truly be sure?

She fidgeted on the seat, angered by her doubts and by the situation that caused them. "Listen, Blake, are you heading home right now? If you are, I would really like to meet your friend, Steven."

"Actually, we just pulled into the driveway, but I can ask him. Hold on."

There was muffled dialogue, as though Blake had put his hand over the phone. He came back a second later.

"Sorry, Mrs. Cheryl. Steven is headed back to Wellington tonight. He says he has a meeting with some kids he can't miss." He laughed, as though he and Steven were in on a joke only they could understand.

Suspicion grew in Cheryl's head. What kind of meeting? Was that how he passed drugs to kids—by meeting with them on weekends and after school?

"Okay, well, I'm sorry to miss him. Maybe we can meet another time."

"Sure. Listen, I've gotta go. I promised my dad that I would get changed and head straight over to the barn."

"All right. Thanks, Blake."

"Bye."

He hung up, and Cheryl stared at her phone for a long moment. She was no closer to finding out who was supplying the drugs to the kids in Sugarcreek, but now she at least had a solid lead.

Tucking her phone into her purse, she climbed from the car and headed back into the station. Esther sat waiting on the chairs outside Chief Twitchell's office, her face red and her eyes puffy from crying.

She looked up as Cheryl approached and stood. "I'm all finished. Chief Twitchell said it was all right for me to go home."

"Good. I've got just one more thing I need to do." She handed her the car keys. "Would you mind waiting for me in the car? I'll be out in just a moment."

"Okay."

Chief Twitchell stepped out of his office. Esther threw a timid glance at him and another at Delores before hurrying out the door.

Cheryl gestured toward the chief's office. "May I speak with you a moment?"

"Of course." He pushed the door open wider. "Come on in."

"Thanks, Chief."

Cheryl let her purse strap slip from her shoulder as she sank into the chair opposite his desk. "I take it everything went okay with Esther?"

He nodded. "She was much more forthcoming."

Relief filled her. "Good. Thank you for letting her go home tonight."

He shrugged and dropped into his chair. "I didn't see the point in holding her. She's not a flight risk. Besides, I think she's told me everything she knows about the drugs, which wasn't a whole lot." He dropped his gaze and looked at his notes. "I will be bringing the boy in, Zachary Waller, for questioning."

"So then, Esther *did* confirm that he was the one who gave her the drugs?"

He nodded and reached up to scratch his temple. "Hard to imagine a person being gullible enough to take a bag from someone without knowing what's inside."

So, then the choices were either Esther was naive or she was lying. She hated to think she could have been lying, but neither did she believe her naive. Lying would mean she was protecting Zach—or maybe Blake. Much as she hated to admit it, both were a possibility.

Her mind made up, she leaned forward and placed her hand on the desk. "Listen, Chief, you may also want to talk to a boy named Blake Dorman. He and his family are staying at our farm."

His eyebrows rose. "Why? What connection does he have to any of this?"

She swallowed the apprehensive knot that rose in her throat. "Esther...she called him a little while ago. I think they might have been talking about the bag."

"Any reason why you would suspect it wasn't just a friendly call?"

A sick feeling settled in Cheryl's stomach. "He...well...he did have some trouble with drugs at his last school. His parents told us they moved here to get him away from all of that."

He nodded and jotted the name down on his notepad. "Okay. What else?"

"Just one other thing." She paused and lowered her voice. "I think Esther has a pretty deep crush on Zach. That could be why she wasn't forthcoming at first—she may have been trying to protect him. You might want to keep that in mind when you talk to her again."

He grunted and tipped his chair onto two legs. "I figured as much. Seems like there's always a boy involved when girls as sweet as Esther find themselves in a heap of trouble."

She blew out a breath, wishing she could blow out the unpleasant feelings rolling around in her stomach so easily. "So what's next?"

"Well, like I said, we'll bring the Waller boy in for questioning, though according to Esther, we're not likely to get much out of him. I'll talk to his parents, find out who his friends are, that sort of thing."

"But you're not holding out much hope that it will lead to anything."

"Not really." The chair settled to the floor with a thump. "I did some checking. Waller's father is an attorney. His mother comes from old money. They know how to protect themselves."

Cheryl frowned. "What does that mean for Henry?"

"For now, he stays where he is. To be honest, I really don't think sitting in a cell will change his mind at all, but I'm hopin' it will at least give him time to think, and maybe it'll force someone else to come forward if they think he might end up paying for something he didn't do. After that, I'll check with some friends up near Wellington and see what I can find out about the Dorman kid."

Cheryl sighed and moved to rise. "Okay. Well, thanks so much for your help, Chief."

"You got it, Cheryl. And..." He waited until she swung around to look at him and then flashed a knowing grin. "Let me know if you find out anything else, would you?"

She gave a wry grin back. "Will do. Later, Chief."

Esther was quiet on the ride home. She stared out the window, her fingers plucking at the strings on her prayer kapp. Finally, Cheryl broke the silence.

"I tried calling Zach." Esther glanced at her, and Cheryl motioned toward her phone. "The last number dialed. I thought it would be Zach. Blake answered. Do you know why?"

Esther shrugged. "Zach said he lost his phone. He was borrowing Blake's."

Was she telling the truth? It pained Cheryl to realize she didn't know. She turned her gaze to the road.

Levi was waiting for them on the porch when Cheryl pulled into the driveway, but so were Seth and Naomi. Esther let out a deep sigh when she spotted them.

Cheryl reached out and clasped her hand. "Would you like me to talk to them first?"

Esther hesitated then shook her head. "You told me to be up front with them. I should have listened. None of this mess would have happened if I had."

"Well it's not too late." She gave her fingers a squeeze. "Levi and I will give you some time to clear things up with them."

"Danki."

The door handle clacked, and then Esther climbed from the car and made her way slowly up the steps to her parents. Catching

Levi's eye, Cheryl motioned toward the pasture. He joined her there. They stood side by side, looking out over the lush rolling hills, their arms braced on the top fence rail.

"You got my message?"

He nodded.

"Where's Rebecca?"

"Elizabeth took her over to the farm so we could talk. We thought it would be better than having her here."

Cheryl agreed then took a deep breath and explained everything that had happened since she called.

"So Chief Twitchell will be questioning Zach?" he asked.

"And Blake." The sick feeling returned full force. She pushed away from the fence and clutched the top rail in both hands. "I hated telling the chief about the trouble he had back in Wellington."

He squeezed her fingers gently. "You had no choice."

"No, I guess not, but I still wish there was another way."

Levi tipped his head back toward the house. "It looks like Esther is leaving. We should go and talk to Maam and Daed. I am sure they will have questions."

"Yeah, I'm sure they will."

A tear dripped from Esther's chin as she passed, and Cheryl stifled a flash of anger toward Zach. A broken heart was hard for anyone, but adding legal troubles just made the whole thing so much worse.

Naomi met them at the porch and held out her hands to Cheryl. "Danki for calling to warn us what was happening with Esther."

"Of course." Cheryl's gaze slid to Seth. "She told you what happened?"

Seth nodded and motioned to a set of rocking chairs next to the porch swing. "Come. We should sit. We have much to discuss."

Leaving the rocking chairs for Seth and Naomi, Cheryl perched on the swing next to Levi.

"Well, speaking of warnings, I should probably tell you to expect another visit from Chief Twitchell. He's going to be questioning people while he tries to figure out where the drugs are coming from," Cheryl said.

Seth gave a slow nod. Cheryl glanced at Levi.

"And he'll probably be stopping by here to talk to Blake."

Levi leaned forward to rest his elbows against his knees, pushing the swing into gentle motion. "All right. I will speak to Kyle and let him know."

"Thank you."

"In the meantime…" Naomi glanced at her husband and then Cheryl and Levi. "Perhaps we should take some time to pray for everyone involved, especially our Esther." She shook her head sadly. "This is so unlike her."

"We are all subject to the beguilement of the enemy," Seth said, "even our Esther. I should have been more watchful where she is concerned. She is my responsibility."

"Do not blame yourself, Daed," Levi said gently. "Esther is no longer a child. She makes her own choices." He glanced at Naomi. "But I think you are right, Maam. We should pray for her, and for the boys as well."

He looked at Cheryl and put out his hand. When she took it, he bowed his head and began praying. Cheryl's heart warmed listening to him. Even the sick feeling in her stomach began to fade as she turned her thoughts and tuned her heart to seeking God. When Levi mentioned Blake, Cheryl felt especially compelled to pray. What was it about him that filled her spirit with such urgency?

At the "amen," Cheryl lifted her head. To her surprise, Wilma stood at the corner of the house, a basket of laundry held to her hip.

"I'm sorry. I didn't mean to intrude, but I couldn't help overhearing." She stepped closer, her eyes wide and frightened. She shifted the basket, her gaze bouncing from Cheryl to Levi. "Did I hear you mention Blake?"

Cheryl started to pull her hand away from Levi, but he kept his grip on her fingers and pushed off the swing with her. "Wilma, we need to talk."

"Why?" She lowered the basket slowly. "What happened? What don't I know?"

CHAPTER TWENTY-THREE

Cheryl crossed the porch, saddened by the worry and fear she read in Wilma's eyes and knowing it would only get worse.

"Hey, Wilma." She motioned toward one of the empty chairs. "Do you have a moment? Levi and I would like to speak with you."

Seth stood, as did Naomi. He put his hand to her back and moved with her to the stairs. "We will let you talk."

Cheryl put her hand out. "Naomi, about Rebecca..."

Naomi shook her head. "Do not worry, Cheryl, I will watch her. Take your time. When you are finished, you and Levi come to the house for supper." She looked at Wilma. "Your family is welcome as well, Wilma."

She nodded hesitantly. "Thank you."

While they crossed the yard toward their own home, Wilma eased toward the porch steps.

"What is going on?" she said. "Is Blake all right?"

"Blake is fine," Cheryl assured her quickly. "But something did happen today that we feel you and Kyle need to be aware of." She glanced down the hill toward the barn. "Is he here? Maybe we should get him."

Wilma shook her head. "No. He took the truck into town. He said he needed to pick up some spark plugs for the tractor. It was running rough."

Cheryl glanced at Levi. This was the first she'd heard of a problem with the tractor, but Kyle was a mechanic. Maybe he knew something they didn't. Levi shrugged, so Cheryl turned her gaze back to Wilma.

"Okay, well why don't we sit down?"

Wilma set the basket down and took one of the chairs, but without something for her hands to do, she wound up wringing them nervously in her lap.

"So, as I said before, something happened today," Cheryl began, "but to be completely honest with you, I really have no idea how deeply Blake is involved, if at all."

Wilma frowned and then motioned for Cheryl to continue. Starting with when she arrived at the store, Cheryl explained everything that had happened. When she finished, Wilma shook her head.

"I don't understand. Why would you think that Blake was involved at all?" she said. "He wasn't at the store."

"No, but you did tell us that drugs were the reason you left Wellington."

Wilma's cheeks colored red. "That's not really fair. All of that happened a long time ago."

"Also, Esther called his phone before we went to the police station," Cheryl continued.

Confusion fluttered across Wilma's face. "Why would she do that?"

"She said it was because he had let someone borrow it," Cheryl said.

Wilma clutched the arms of her chair. "Well, we should ask him. Blake didn't have anything to do with those drugs. I'm sure of it."

"We will speak with Esther again," Levi assured her. "For sure and for certain."

"But in the meantime," Cheryl continued, "I wonder if you wouldn't mind telling me about Blake's friend Steven. Blake said he gave him a ride again today."

Confusion registered on Wilma's face. "Yes, he does that quite a bit. He and Steven are very close."

Cheryl licked her lips, searching for the best way to phrase the question smoldering on her tongue. "Wilma, how well do you know this man?"

Surprise showed in her eyes as she looked from Cheryl to Levi. "Blake certainly knows him better than I do, I suppose. Why?"

She took a deep breath and pressed her hands to her knees. "Wilma, please understand, I am in no way suggesting that Blake is involved with drugs."

Wilma pressed her lips together tightly, her eyes wide. "But?"

Cheryl looked to Levi for encouragement. He nodded. She returned her gaze to Wilma. "Someone is supplying drugs to the kids here in Sugarcreek. Blake said Steven had a meeting with some kids back in Wellington that he couldn't miss. Could he be the person—?"

Wilma was shaking her head before Cheryl could even finish. She even let a small laugh escape—one that likely had more to do with relief than humor. "No, no, no. You don't understand. Blake's friend's name is Steven Croft. He's the youth minister at a church back in Wellington that Blake used to attend."

"A youth minister?" Cheryl and Levi said simultaneously.

Cheryl calculated the distance in her head then frowned. "But Wellington is almost seventy miles away. Why is he driving all the way over here?"

Worry clouded Wilma's gaze. She crossed her legs and bobbed her foot in agitation. "Blake took it really hard when he found out we were moving. I think Steven is just trying to make things a little easier, let him know he's still there for him." Her foot stilled, and she peered earnestly at Cheryl. "You need to understand something. Aside from a couple of his coaches, Steven was the only person who really took the time to get to know Blake. He saw through the moods and anger and showed real love for him. I know he's the reason Blake accepted Christ."

Cheryl listened in shocked silence. "So, the meeting he mentioned?"

Wilma smiled. "There's a large group of kids in Wellington who come from single-parent homes. Once or twice a week, Steven opens the church gym. He plans games, gets them pizza, basically just gives them a place to go. And the parents go to work without worrying what their kids are up to."

Embarrassed by the conclusions she'd jumped to, Cheryl dropped her gaze. "Wow. I was really wrong about him."

Wilma made a *pooh* sound and reached for the laundry basket near her feet. "It's okay. I guess I would have been suspicious of him too if I'd been in your shoes."

As she pushed up to stand, a pair of blue jeans tumbled from the basket onto the porch.

"I'll get those," Cheryl said.

"Oh, that's all right."

Wilma stretched out her hand, but Cheryl had already bent to snag the jeans off the floor. On one leg, a dark red stain marred the denim. Cheryl stared at it curiously. It almost looked like...

Blood?

"Thanks, Cheryl. I'll take those." Wilma grabbed the jeans from her and shoved them deep into the basket. The movement caused her sleeve to ride farther up her arm, exposing a nasty-looking bruise as big as Cheryl's hand.

"Wilma, what happened to your arm?" Cheryl said, her eyes widening.

Wilma followed her gaze to the purplish mark on her arm. "Oh, that." She chuckled wryly and smoothed her sleeve down into place. "I did it moving our stuff the other day. So silly of me. It's really not as bad as it looks. Anyway, I'll talk to you guys later, okay?"

She hurried off the porch toward the clotheslines Levi had strung behind the dawdy haus, the basket jostling on her hip.

Cheryl turned wide eyes to Levi. "Did you see that bruise?"

He ran his fingers over his beard and came to stand beside her. "We *were* doing a lot of lifting, and Kyle said Wilma spent most of the afternoon rearranging furniture."

"Mmm. I guess."

Levi snugged his arm around her waist. "What were you looking at on those jeans?"

Cheryl's thoughts leaped from the bruise on Wilma's arm to the stained jeans. "I only caught a quick glance, but I think it was blood," she said. "There was kind of a reddish, almost blackish stain all over the bottom of one of the legs. Blake didn't hurt himself working on the farm, did he?"

Levi frowned then shook his head. "I don't think so. Not that I saw."

"It was a pretty large stain, Levi. Maybe you should ask him about it."

He smiled and pressed a kiss to the top of her head. "If it will make my wife stop worrying, I will ask."

She laid her hand over his hand on her waist. "Thank you."

"You are welcome." Levi gave her one last kiss then dropped his arm. "I should get back to the barn. Kyle and I were not quite finished when I got your message about Esther."

"Okay. While you're doing that, I'll walk over and pick up Rebecca."

"And maybe talk things over with Maam?" He chuckled and gave Cheryl a wink.

"Obviously, you know me pretty well," she said, smiling back.

The truth was, Cheryl often talked things over with her mother-in-law. They were friends, and friends talked. But this time was different. This time she needed to come clean about everything that had been going on with Esther, and the Dormans, and the drugs. In a nutshell, what she really needed was a dose of Naomi's down-to-earth wisdom.

Chapter Twenty-Four

A steady rain fell all during the night and faded off the next day, midway through the church services, so that by the time Cheryl and Levi returned home for lunch, the entire farm felt scrubbed and freshly washed. As they got out of the car, Rebecca pointed to a mud puddle and began bouncing with excitement on Cheryl's hip.

"*Splaa, splaa!*"

Cheryl tightened her grip. "No, Boo, we aren't going to splash in the puddle."

Rebecca strained against Cheryl's arms. "Momma, *splaa!*"

"Come, little one." Levi took her from Cheryl and swung her up onto his shoulders. "Let's walk down to the barn while Momma starts lunch, ja?"

"Thank you," Cheryl said, blowing out a weary sigh. Handling a toddler required a lot of energy. She had no idea how single parents were able to manage it on their own.

"I'll let you know when it's ready," she said, putting her hand to her mouth and calling down the hill after them.

Levi waved, and Rebecca promptly put both hands in the air to copy him. Cheryl smiled watching them.

Wilma rounded the house, and Rebecca waved to her too. Wilma waved back and then joined Cheryl by the porch. "She certainly loves her daddy."

"Yes, she does. But I'd say the feeling is mutual."

"Oh, I'm sure."

Cheryl turned to look at Wilma. She looked sad...and tired. There were dark smudges under her eyes, and her hair was disheveled.

Cheryl motioned toward the house. "Would you like to come inside, Wilma? I was just about to make lunch. You're welcome to join us."

"Oh, I don't mean to interrupt," Wilma said. "I was just going to ask if you were busy tomorrow."

Cheryl quickly thought over her schedule. "No, I don't have anything special planned. Why? Is there something I can do for you?"

"Actually, it's Blake. Steven is busy so he is going to need a ride into practice. I was hoping, if you didn't mind—"

"Of course I don't mind. I'll be glad to take him," Cheryl said. Plus, spending a few minutes with Blake would give her a chance to ask him if he'd let anyone borrow his phone. "What time does he need to be there?"

"Seven thirty." Wilma's smile showed her relief. "Thank you so much, Cheryl. It's tough getting him back and forth to the school with only one vehicle."

"Well, I'm glad you asked. Any time you or Blake need a ride, don't hesitate, okay?" She motioned toward the house. "Are you sure you and your family wouldn't like to stay for lunch? It's nothing fancy, just some sandwiches and salads, but if you didn't already have something else planned, I could use a hand."

"Oh, well..."

"C'mon," Cheryl urged, turning for the steps. "There's no sense in both of us messing up our kitchens, right?"

Wilma smiled and followed her up onto the porch. "Well, when you put it that way..."

"Good. I'll text Levi and tell him to bring Kyle and Blake with him when he comes."

Cheryl sent the message then led the way to the kitchen. While she pulled the things to make sandwiches out of the refrigerator, Wilma washed her hands, giving Cheryl another look at the bruise on her arm. She hadn't exaggerated how bad it looked in her mind. It was larger than a softball and greenish-blue around the edges. She hid a frown. Wilma said she got it moving, so why was it already starting to change color?

She set a package of turkey and sliced cheese on the counter then pointed to Wilma's arm.

"I've got some ointment that Naomi gave me to use on sore muscles and stuff. Would you like to try some? It might help bring down some of that bruise," she said.

Wilma gave a self-conscious laugh and dried her hands on a towel. "Thanks, but I don't think that's necessary. It really doesn't even hurt."

"Okay, well if you change your mind, let me know."

"Thanks, Cheryl." Wilma reached for the loaf of bread and began removing slices and laying them side by side on the counter. "How shall we do this? Assembly-line style?"

Cheryl laughed. "I like how you think." She handed Wilma the turkey and cheese, then grabbed a butter knife so she could add mustard and mayo. "I'll slice up some tomato and onion and let everyone add their own. Sound good?"

"Perfect."

While they worked, Cheryl and Wilma talked—about things that were happening at the farm, at church, even at Blake's school. Wilma seemed to perk up some, and looked much less careworn by the time the men came in for lunch.

"Momma, Momma!" Rebecca stormed through the door first, her tiny feet stomping with excitement as she told Cheryl all about the things she'd seen and done in the barn.

While the men washed up, Cheryl swung Rebecca up to sit on the counter so she could wipe the dirt from her face and hands. "It sounds like you had so much fun, Boo."

Rebecca grimaced as Cheryl ran a damp paper towel over her face. A string of syllables came out of her and then—"Ranger!"

Laughter broke out at her enthusiastic chatter.

Putting her finger to Rebecca's lips, Cheryl whispered, "Inside voice, little one." She shot a glance at Levi. "Did you take her riding? In her church clothes?"

He grinned and pointed to Blake. "Not me. Blake took her."

"I was very careful, Mrs. Cheryl. She sat on Ranger's back while I walked beside her and held her steady."

Cheryl laughed and set Rebecca on her feet. "Well, she can be pretty convincing. Thank you for humoring her." She motioned toward the food on the counter. "How about we make our sandwiches in here and carry them to the dining room?"

Kyle rubbed his hands together. "Good idea. I'm starving. Thanks again for inviting us."

Cheryl smiled and handed him a plate. "No problem. I'm glad you all could join us."

Talk continued while they made their sandwiches and seated themselves around the table to eat. All except for Wilma. The moment the men showed up, she fell back into her reserved manner and spoke only when someone asked her a direct question. Once the meal was over, she quickly rose and began clearing the table.

"I can do that, Wilma," Cheryl said, pushing her chair back.

She shook her head and continued clearing plates. "It's no trouble. I want to help."

Rebecca began fussing, so Levi stood and plucked her from her high chair. "Let's go sit on the swing, okay, my Rebecca? Kyle, would you like to join us?"

Kyle started to rise, but stopped when Blake cleared his throat.

"Don't forget, I need the truck keys so I can go by the field house today. We're studying game film from last year."

Kyle glanced uneasily at Levi then back at Blake. "On a Sunday?"

"I'm new. Coach really wants me to study the films so I can get an idea of the offense he runs."

"I don't like it, Blake—"

"Dad." Blake braced both hands on the tabletop. "I told you about this last week. Sunday afternoons are the only days I can get in there. We have practice every other day, and when I'm not at practice, I have to help out on the farm."

A flush crept over Kyle's cheeks, and his stare became more pointed. "It's called earning a living, son, not 'helping.' The Millers here have been kind enough to give us a place to live. Working the farm is the least we can do."

"The least *you* can do," Blake muttered.

"Blake," Wilma urged. Her hands began shaking, rattling the dishes she had gathered.

Cheryl stood. "Here, Wilma, I'll take those."

The family obviously needed a moment of privacy. She gave a look to Levi, who nodded and quietly let himself out the front door with Rebecca in his arms. Cheryl ducked into the kitchen and turned on the water to drown out the conversation happening in the dining room. After a moment, the front door closed, hard. Was it Blake who had left, or Kyle? Or both?

Cheryl shut off the water and returned to the dining room. "So, is everything all right—?"

She broke off, stunned by what she saw. Wilma stood pressed against the wall, a grimace twisting her lips. Next to her, Kyle clutched her by the arm, his face angry and red. He stepped away quickly at Cheryl's appearance and moved out the door without a word.

Cheryl turned wide eyes to Wilma. "Are...are you all right? What just happened?"

Her gaze fell to Wilma's arm—the same arm that bore the ugly bruise. A hand-sized bruise, she realized now. One likely belonging to a man.

Wilma rubbed it gingerly with her other hand and gave a small laugh. "Don't...don't get the wrong idea, Cheryl. That wasn't what it looked like."

Cheryl rushed to her. "Then what was it? Because it looked like...like..."

She trailed off, unable to voice the thought crashing through her brain. Blowing out a sharp breath, she jammed her fists on her hips and looked Wilma in the eyes.

"Wilma, what happened to your arm? You didn't do it moving, did you?" she said, accusation ringing in her voice. She didn't wait for an answer but jerked her head angrily toward the door. "Did Kyle do that? Because judging from what I just saw—"

Wilma jerked away from the wall and grabbed Cheryl's hand. "No, Cheryl. It wasn't Kyle." She took a quivering breath then shook her head. "You're right. I didn't get this bruise moving furniture. But it wasn't Kyle who did it either."

Cheryl's eyes widened. "What are you saying, Wilma? If it wasn't Kyle, then...who?"

Misery clouded Wilma's gaze. A tremor shook her, and she closed her eyes a long moment then opened them again slowly. "It was Blake, Cheryl. Blake gave me this bruise."

CHAPTER TWENTY-FIVE

Cheryl flipped the car heater to high while she waited for Blake to emerge from the dawdy haus so she could drive him to practice. It was summer, but on this particular morning, a dampness floated on the air and settled deep into her bones.

Of course, it didn't help that she was also tired and cranky.

She flicked on the wipers and swished away the dew from the windows. She had tossed and turned most of the night, going over and over the story Wilma had shared about her argument with Blake. She claimed she'd been standing on a chair hanging curtains when it happened—and that she'd spun to give a sharp retort and would have fallen had Blake not caught her arm. Of course, that didn't explain the sneaking suspicion brewing in Cheryl's brain that the bruise was actually much older.

As for Kyle, Wilma said that he'd only just noticed the bruise when Cheryl walked in. The anger she'd witnessed from him was in response to what he deemed as carelessness on her part and Blake's for inspiring the argument in the first place.

Cheryl sighed and drummed her fingers against the steering wheel. Levi had seemed to think Wilma's explanation was reasonable, but she wasn't so sure, especially after a night spent tossing and turning until the wee hours. It wasn't until she'd spent some time praying over the situation that she was finally able to drift off to sleep.

Thinking of her prayer reminded her of what she'd determined when she woke up. God's word said men looked on the outward appearance, but He looked on the heart. In other words, she needed to try and get to know Blake's heart. The only way to do that would be to spend time with him, getting to know him better. Fortunately, driving him to practice provided her with the perfect opportunity, but not if she had a daughter in tow.

Naomi agreed, and had volunteered to keep Rebecca so that Cheryl could speak to him without interruption. That was probably a good thing. Blake had to be at the field house by seven thirty, and Rebecca wouldn't like being awakened early after the late night they'd had. A cranky toddler would hardly have allowed them to talk.

The door opened and Blake stepped out, his gym bag slung over his shoulder.

"Blake! Your cleats!" Wilma called.

He rolled his eyes and dropped his bag on the porch, then held up one finger to Cheryl, indicating he'd return in a just a minute. She nodded and waved him off. A second later, the door opened again, but this time it was Kyle who came out. He had a brown lunch bag in his hand. Bending down, he unzipped Blake's bag, dropped the lunch sack inside, then re-zipped the bag and loped off the porch toward her car. Cheryl rolled down the window.

"Morning, Mrs. Miller."

"Good morning, Kyle."

He hitched his thumb toward the house. "I was just giving Blake his lunch. The kid would forget his head if it weren't attached."

Cheryl laughed. "Typical teenager."

When Blake stepped onto the porch, Kyle patted the side of her car. "There he is. Thanks for giving him a ride today."

"No problem. Glad to do it."

He moved off, but as he did, Cheryl noticed something. Kyle was wearing the stained blue jeans that had fallen from Wilma's laundry basket.

Blake interrupted her musings with a cheery, "Hey, Mrs. Cheryl." He tossed the gym bag onto the floor behind the passenger seat and then climbed into the car.

Cheryl cast one last glance at Kyle's stained jeans in the driver's door mirror before turning to smile at Blake. "Good morning, Blake."

She dropped the car into Reverse and backed down the driveway.

"Thanks again for the ride," he said, clicking his seat belt into place. "Steven was supposed to come, but he had a staff meeting at the church he had to go to."

"No problem. I don't mind at all." She smiled and shot him a glance. "So how did the film study go?"

He shrugged. "Okay, I guess. Coach runs a spread option offense, which is different from what we used to run at Wellington. I'm getting the hang of it, but breaking old habits is hard."

"Well, considering that I didn't understand a word of what you just said, I'd say you're way ahead of me."

He smiled wryly and relaxed against the seat. "Not into football?"

"I enjoy watching it, but I confess, I'm not super savvy when it comes to all the rules."

He nodded and fell silent.

Cheryl focused on the road, her finger tapping the steering wheel. "So, Blake, tell me about your friend Steven. Your mom told me he's a youth minister?"

"Yep."

Ugh. One syllable answers were hardly a conversation. She tried again. "What church did you meet him at?"

Blake lifted an eyebrow. "Oh, I didn't meet him at church. I met him at the school. He used to come by during my lunch period to eat with some of the kids from his youth group."

Much better. Now they were talking. She smiled. "I didn't realize the school allowed that."

He shrugged. "Just like any other visitor, I guess."

"Hmm. I guess so. And you two got to be friends?"

He grew more animated as his excitement grew. "Oh, yeah. He's really an awesome guy. He used to come to all my games, give me rides to church, all kinds of stuff."

"And he visits you in Sugarcreek." She looked over at him. "Isn't that kinda far for him to drive?"

He thought for a second then hitched one shoulder. "Well, I guess that's just because he wanted to see how things were going with my dad."

He stopped and shot a glance at her. Something about the way he did it made Cheryl think he regretted what he'd just said.

222 | Sugarcreek Amish Mysteries

"Have things been tough between you and your dad before?" she asked quietly. Fearing he might not answer, she kept her gaze on the road ahead.

"Dad is pretty set in his ways. We argue about that a lot."

He said no more, and Cheryl suspected he would keep it that way. They arrived at the school a short while later, and she had yet to ask about his phone. She pulled into a parking space and then motioned toward his bag. "Call me if you need anything. You still have my number?"

"Yeah, I've got it." He reached for the strap on the duffel and gave it a tug.

"Blake, before you go, do you mind if I ask if you've let anyone borrow your phone lately? Maybe Zach, or someone else from the team?"

He shrugged. "Yeah, I let people borrow it, when their battery dies and stuff like that. Why?"

"Just curious." She smiled and waved goodbye after promising to return to pick him up around noon.

In the meantime, she grabbed her phone and searched Steven Croft's name. She quickly pulled up a link that listed him as the youth minister at a church in Wellington called Living Hope. She memorized the number then backed out of the parking lot and headed toward Yoder's Corner for coffee and a warm cinnamon roll.

August Yoder greeted her at the door with a cheery smile. "Good morning, Cheryl." He held up a menu. "Do you want to look, or are you having your usual?"

She groaned. "Are cinnamon rolls my usual? If so, I may need to go on a diet."

"Nonsense." August's wife, Greta, slapped his arm and pushed past him. "You're already too thin." She handed Cheryl an empty coffee cup then motioned toward the tables. "Sit anywhere. I'll bring you some coffee."

"Okay. Thanks, Greta."

Even though she'd teased, Cheryl ended up ordering a roll to go with her coffee. While she waited for Greta to bring it, she took out her phone and dialed the number to the church. It went straight to voice mail, and Cheryl realized that at only seven forty, it was probably much too early for anyone to be there. She settled back and enjoyed her breakfast before trying again.

"Living Hope. This is Tammy speaking. May I help you?"

Cheryl pushed up in the booth and ran a napkin over her mouth. "Good morning. Is Steven Croft available?"

"Yes, he is. May I tell him who's calling?"

"This is Cheryl Miller."

"Hold on a moment, Ms. Miller."

A buzz sounded, and then a male voice answered, "This is Steven."

"Mr. Croft? Hi. My name is Cheryl Miller. My husband and I own the farm where Blake Dorman and his family are staying."

"Oh. Hi, Mrs. Miller. Blake has told me a lot about you."

"He has?"

"Absolutely." She heard the smile in his voice. "He really likes you and your family. Your husband's name is Levi?"

"Yes, that's right."

"Blake really looks up to him. Talks about him all the time. He said he's teaching him a lot about farming."

"I didn't realize Blake was all that interested in farming. To be honest, I assumed he thought it was all pretty boring."

Greta walked up with a pot of coffee. Seeing Cheryl was on the phone, she held it up and lifted her eyebrows, but stayed quiet. Cheryl shook her head, and Greta moved off to offer the coffee to the next customer.

"I don't think Blake knows what he's interested in. He's still in that 'trying to figure it all out' stage."

"Oh, yeah. We all go through that at one time or another."

"Yeah." He gave a small chuckle, then fell silent. "So, how can I help you today?"

"You're probably wondering why I'm calling," she said at almost the same moment. "Oh, sorry."

"No problem." The warmth in his voice faded. "Mrs. Miller, is everything okay with Blake? I mean, is that why you're calling?"

"Oh, yes. Everything is fine."

Which wasn't exactly true, considering she still didn't know if Blake was the person bringing drugs into Sugarcreek. She frowned and started again.

"Look, I realize you don't know me, but I've been a little worried about something Blake said, and I'm wondering if maybe you could help."

"I can try," he said, uncertainty registering in his voice. "What exactly was it he said?"

She picked up her fork and dragged the tines through the frosting left on her plate from the cinnamon roll. "Well, I understand he and his father tend to argue quite a bit?"

He was quiet for a moment, and then said, "Did Blake tell you that?"

"He did, though he probably didn't have to. I've sorta figured that out just watching the interaction between the two of them."

He grunted. "Yeah. Blake and his dad don't exactly see eye to eye."

"Blake said you come to Sugarcreek to check on him?"

He gave another grunt.

She set down the fork. "Why is that, if you don't mind my asking? I mean, apart from just being a good friend, is there something else that brings you here?"

He was quiet for so long, Cheryl thought they might have been disconnected.

"Look, Mrs. Miller," he said at last, "Blake is a really good kid. I mean, I know he's had problems in the past, but he's trying really hard to change all of that. His dad..."

His voice took on a hard edge. He cleared his throat and started again. "His dad hasn't always been the most supportive. Worse, I think Blake used to really be afraid of him."

She paused. "It's sort of typical to be afraid of your parents, isn't it?" she asked carefully.

"You don't understand. I'm not talking about the normal, everyday, respect-your-parents kind of fear," he said. "Blake used to come to church with bruises. Bad ones. I asked him about it, but he always insisted they came from football practice."

"And you didn't believe him?"

He was quiet for another lengthy spell. Finally, he sighed. "I didn't have a reason *not* to."

Odd choice of words. It was as if by his denial, he was voicing his apprehension.

"But you suspected his father," she guessed, and knew she was right when he stayed silent. "Why?"

He paused. "Gut instinct, I guess. Something just didn't feel right. Unfortunately, you can't report a 'feeling.'"

He'd been worried enough to consider filing a report?

She squeezed the phone. "You were really worried, weren't you?"

He didn't answer, so Cheryl pressed on. "What about Blake's mother? Did you ever notice any bruises on her?"

"Not that I saw," he said quickly. "I mean, I saw plenty of other problems between the two of them, arguments and stuff like that, but nothing physical."

"Okay." She thought hard for a second, then said, "Would you mind if I asked one more thing?"

"Sure."

"Sorry, hold on one second."

An older couple entered the restaurant. Cheryl fidgeted nervously while they passed by her table. When they were out of earshot, she said, "The phone Blake carries is pretty expensive. Do you happen to know where he got it?"

Though she couldn't see him, she could feel his disapproval, and sensed him pulling away.

"He didn't steal it, Mrs. Miller. Is that what you're asking?"

"I didn't mean it like that, exactly..."

His voice became hard, his words clipped. "Blake's grandfather gave him that phone. I think he was worried about him—wanted him to have a way to get in touch in case—"

Intrigued, Cheryl leaned forward. "In case...what?"

Steven cleared his throat. "Please, forget I said that. I got carried away."

Disappointment settled in Cheryl's chest at the note of finality in Steven's voice. Obviously, he was loyal to Blake and wouldn't betray his trust. "I'm sorry. I'm a little frustrated, but I shouldn't have pressed."

He blew out a sigh. "That's okay."

Before they disconnected, there was one more thing Cheryl wanted to say. She brought the phone closer to her mouth and turned her face to the window.

"Listen, I think it's really great that you kept in touch with Blake. I know it means a lot to him. My husband and I work with the youth here in Sugarcreek, so I can appreciate how much time and effort you're investing."

Interest flared in his voice. "Oh yeah? That's awesome."

"Well, we're just sponsors," she said. "We mostly help out the youth minister with food and chaperones and stuff like that when he asks."

"I've got a few couples here in Wellington who do the same kind of thing. They're great. Makes my job a lot easier since we have such a large group of students meeting here on Wednesday nights."

"But you still make time to help Blake? That's pretty impressive."

"He's worth it. Like I said, he's a good kid."

"He seems like it. And it's great that you're willing to help him turn his life around."

"I'm sorry... I'm not sure what you mean."

The confusion was back. She heard it in his voice.

"I just mean about the drugs," Cheryl said. "His parents told us the reason they left Wellington was because he'd gotten mixed up with them."

"They said that?" Steven's voice cracked, and she heard him straining to stay calm. "Mrs. Miller, Blake has never done drugs a day in his life."

Chapter Twenty-Six

B lake hates drugs, Mrs. Miller," Steven continued, firmly. "He and I have talked about it a lot. It's something he's passionate about. In fact, after a friend of his overdosed at a party, Blake talked about starting a care group for students whose families were battling drug addiction."

Cheryl blinked in confusion as the memory of the exchange between Blake and Zach flashed before her eyes. "But...I saw..."

"Whatever you saw," he said gently, "it didn't have anything to do with drugs. I'd stake my life on it."

He sounded so certain, Cheryl felt her own opinion waver. "That's good to know." She licked her lips nervously. "Anyway, thanks for your help today. I really appreciate you talking with me."

"No problem. Oh, and Mrs. Miller? You said you and your husband work with youth?"

"Yes, that's right."

"I'm really glad to hear that. I've been praying for Blake, ever since he first told me his family was moving. I've been hoping God would make sure he got into a good place with good influences around him. I'm really glad to hear He answered that prayer."

Humbled by his words, Cheryl dipped her head. "Wow. That's...I mean, thank you."

"You're welcome. And if you wouldn't mind, could you kinda keep an eye on Blake? He's a good kid and all, but he's had a rough time with his dad. I'd hate to see him go astray now."

"I'll do my best."

"Thank you. God bless, okay?"

"You too."

She hung up, her thoughts in a whirl. Steven was adamant that Blake was not involved with drugs. But Zach certainly had something to do with them. Either he'd been giving the drugs to Esther, or he'd been picking them up. So, if Blake wasn't the one supplying Zach with them, then who was? And what had they been talking about the day she saw them outside of Weaver Lumber?

Giving a sigh of frustration, Cheryl pushed her empty coffee cup away and rummaged in her purse for a piece of paper. Sometimes, jotting things down helped her focus. Finding an old bank envelope, she tore it open and smoothed it flat, then began scribbling everything she knew about the drugs so far. Both times it had been marijuana. Both times, Zach had either been nearby or he'd just left. Also, Chief Twitchell seemed certain that kids were involved, another tidbit that also pointed to Zach. Then again, Zach had been here all along while the Dormans had only recently come to the area.

She paused, put the tip of her pen between her teeth, and stared at what she'd written. In all of this, the two people she'd never considered were Kyle and Wilma. Then again, she'd never had reason to suspect them. Or did she?

Quickly, she scribbled their names. Next to them she wrote, *lied about why they came to Sugarcreek* and underlined it. Of course, there were any number of explanations as to why they could have come. Was lying reason enough to suspect one or both of them of drug dealing?

She wadded up the envelope, but stopped herself shy of throwing it away. Maybe lying about their reasons for moving to Sugarcreek wasn't such a big deal, but then again, if they hadn't told them the truth about that, what else had they lied about?

Drawing a breath, she unwadded the paper and smoothed it again on the table. If there was a golden rule of mystery solving, it was to look at every suspect objectively, assuming nothing.

She clicked her pen and next to Kyle's name she wrote— bloodstains. What bloodstains had to do with anything, she had no idea, but it was unusual, and so she would include it. She also added *temper* and *bruises* to the list.

She fiddled with the pen and then froze as another thought struck. The spark plugs. Wilma had said Kyle had gone into town to buy new ones because the tractor was running rough, but Levi hadn't known anything about it.

She grabbed her phone and looked at the time. Only nine thirty. It was still early, and Levi was likely to be in the field or in the barn. Still, she punched the phone icon and dialed the number to the house.

"Hello?"

She startled. "You answered."

"Ja, because you called."

"Never mind." She waved her hand and bent her head over the phone. "Levi, are you in the barn?"

"Ne, but I can head that way. What is wrong?"

"Do you remember the spark plugs Wilma said Kyle went into town to buy? Can you check to see if he actually changed them on the tractor?"

"I suppose," he said uncertainly. "But why? Is something wrong?"

"I'm not sure," she said, biting her lip. "I just want to know."

"I will go now. Do you want me to call you back?"

"No, I'll wait."

"Cheryl, did you need something?" Greta sidled up to the table and peered at her curiously. When she didn't answer, Greta tipped her head toward Cheryl's hands. "I saw you waving."

Cheryl blinked in confusion. "What? Oh, no, I wasn't waving at you. I was waving...I mean, I was talking to Levi and I waved. I do that sometimes."

"Okay. Well, I'm here. Can I get you anything else?" She pointed to Cheryl's empty cup. "More coffee?"

Cheryl shook her head. "No, I'm good, thanks."

"Okay, well, holler if you change your mind," Greta said, moving away with a knowing chuckle.

Cheryl sighed. "Hurry, Levi," she muttered.

"I am here."

She tensed at his voice. "Okay, so does it look like Kyle did any work to the tractor?"

"Hold on." She heard some clunking and moving about. Finally, Levi grunted and returned to the phone. "That is odd."

"What is?" She leaned forward, holding her breath.

"Well, from what I can tell," Levi said, his breaths coming in puffs as though he were still bent over the engine and poking about, "it doesn't look like any work has been done to the tractor at all."

Chapter Twenty-Seven

Cheryl sat back against the booth. "No work at all? Are you sure?"

"None that I can tell," Levi said. "Would you like me to ask him?"

"No!" She lowered her voice and cupped her free hand over the phone. "No, don't worry about it. Listen, I'm going to check on something, and then I'll be home, okay?"

"Cheryl." Warning rang in his voice. "What are you up to? What is going on?"

"Don't worry. I'll be home soon. Love you."

She listened for his "I love you too" then disconnected and motioned toward Greta.

"This time, I am waving," she said when she approached. She handed her some money and then reached for her purse. "Thanks, Greta."

Greta glanced down at the ten-dollar bill in her hand. "Don't you want some change?"

"No time. Thanks anyway." Cheryl gave a final wave, then headed out the door and drove across town to the high school, thinking through her plan.

Now that the sun was fully up, the chill was gone from the air. By the time she hurried across the parking lot and then to the practice field, she even felt a few tiny beads of sweat forming on her scalp. Most of the boys were on the far end of the field taking turns with the tackling dummies. Cheryl slowed when she saw them, but both the boys and their coaches were so focused on the drills, they paid no attention to her.

She breathed a relieved sigh and eased over toward the benches, where it looked like most of the players had tossed their gym bags on the ground. She pulled a couple of the Ziplocs she used for Rebecca's snacks from her purse and began to pick blackberries, working her way to the gym bags. Blake's was easy to spot with its distinctive red stripe. It was from his old school back in Wellington. She crossed to it and tugged it free from the pile. Before she actually pulled the zipper open, she hesitated. What she was doing was worse than just snooping. Did she really have any right to go looking through Blake's things? On the other hand, how would she know if the bag she'd seen Kyle stuffing inside really did contain just lunch, as he'd claimed?

Her resolve returning, Cheryl reached for the zipper. Giving a quick flick, she pulled it back. The bag Kyle had left was still on top. She grabbed it and shoved it into her purse, then zipped Blake's gym bag closed. As she straightened, she heard one of the coaches blow a whistle. The football players scattered and some of them started back toward the benches.

Cheryl turned back to the blackberries and resumed gathering the plentiful fruit as Blake neared the benches.

Like most of the other players, Blake was wearing a practice jersey with the sleeves removed. He grabbed a paper cup, filled it with water from a bright orange cooler, swallowed it in one large gulp, then tossed the cup to the ground and headed over to her.

"Hey, Mrs. Cheryl. We're not through with practice yet."

"No, no. I didn't think so." She motioned to his shoulder, where a large bruise peeked out from under the jersey. "Blake, what happened there?"

He glanced at it and then gave a casual shrug. "Eh, it's nothing. I probably got it in tackling practice."

"That's 'cause he's soft, eh, Dorman?" one of the other players scoffed, to which several others joined in teasing laughter.

Blake ignored them and turned back to Cheryl. "Is everything okay?"

"Yes. I noticed these blackberries the other day when I dropped you off. I thought I'd swing by and pick some to take home to make a pie."

"Dorman!" One of the coaches motioned to him. Blake jerked and raised his hand.

"Coming!" He shook his head. "Sorry, Mrs. Cheryl, I have to go."

"Of course. See you after practice."

He jogged off, and Cheryl finished filling her baggie with the fattest blackberries from the brambles. It was then she noticed the juice trickling over her fingers and down her palms—leaving dark, purplish-black stains that looked like—

Blood!

Cheryl stared at her hands. "It wasn't bloodstains on Kyle's jeans, it was blackberry juice."

Her heart thumped hard in her chest. There was only one way those stains could have gotten on his jeans, and that was if he'd been here, right where she was standing.

Suddenly, she remembered Kyle saying he'd been to the practice field, but he claimed it had been when they'd signed Blake up to play.

Scrubbing her hands on the ground, she removed as much of the juice as she could and then reached into her purse for the brown bag she'd taken from Blake's gym bag. Her hands shook as she unrolled the top. She was almost afraid to look, afraid of what she would find, but desperate to know the truth, she stuck her hand inside and pulled out...

CHAPTER TWENTY-EIGHT

I t's drugs, Chief Twitchell. I saw Kyle put them there myself."
Cheryl bent down and patted the bag on top of Chief
Twitchell's desk. Her excitement had kept her from sitting as he'd
requested, and now she paced the room, a bundle of nervous energy.

"Anyway, I was going to give him a ride—"

"Who?"

"Blake, but he forgot his cleats, so he went back into the
house."

"All right now, slow down," the chief said, holding up his
hands. "And start from the beginning. You say you saw Kyle with
this bag?"

"Oh. Right. I've gotten ahead of myself." Drawing a breath,
Cheryl forced herself to speak slowly and calmly, starting from
that morning when she'd picked up Blake for practice, and ending
with the moment she'd pulled the drugs from the brown bag she'd
taken from his gym bag.

"Blake. As in Blake Dorman?" Chief Twitchell removed his
notepad from his desk and flipped past a couple of pages. "Isn't
that the boy you told me had a drug problem back in Wellington?"

Heat flooded Cheryl's cheeks. "Yes, I did say that," she admitted.
"But I was wrong, Chief. Blake never had a drug problem. He lost

one of his friends to drugs. His father only said that because he was trying to cover up his own crimes."

She leaned over the desk and jabbed the notepad with her finger. "I bet the only reason Kyle made his family move from Wellington is because he was afraid he would be caught. And that's not all."

She explained about the bruises she'd spotted on Wilma and then on Blake. "I'm pretty sure he's been threatening them, Chief. Forcing them to keep quiet through physical violence."

"Now, now, let's not jump to any conclusions."

"I'm not the only who thinks so," she said, and filled him in on everything she'd learned from Steven Croft.

The more she talked, the more somber Chief Twitchell became. Finally, he gave a nod and pushed up from behind his desk.

"All right, you've made your case. I'll drive out to the farm and speak to Mr. Dorman myself."

Dismay washed over her. "Speak to him? But, Chief, all that's going to do is warn him that we're onto him."

He held up his hand. "'Fraid I can't do much more than that, Cheryl. At least, not without a warrant."

"Okay, hold on." She thought hard. "Levi and I own the house. Can we give you permission to search?"

He shook his head. "Sorry. No one can give permission except the tenant, or in this case, his spouse."

His spouse. That meant Wilma. Cheryl frowned as she considered the possibility. Wilma loved her son, but would she turn in her husband in order to protect him?

She bit her lip. "Let me talk to her, Chief. Maybe she'd be more inclined to cooperate if I spoke to her first."

He considered this for a long moment, and then nodded. "All right. Let's go."

The drive out to the farm took far longer than the drive in—at least, that's what it felt like to Cheryl. Fortunately, there was still some time before lunch, so Kyle was nowhere near the dawdy haus when she pulled in with Chief Twitchell. He stayed in the car while she went up to the door to knock.

Wilma answered, her hair in limp straggles and her face devoid of makeup. "Hi, Cheryl." She pushed open the screen door and then glanced over Cheryl's shoulder. Spying the chief, her curiosity quickly changed to concern. "What's...uh...what's going on?"

Cheryl motioned toward the house. "Wilma, we need to talk. Would you mind if I came in for a minute?"

Confusion flickered in her eyes, but she nodded and stepped back from the door, then moved toward the living room.

"Let's sit in here."

Cheryl agreed. Sitting would most definitely be good, especially when she told Wilma they needed to search the house.

Screwing up her courage, Cheryl dove into their reason for coming. The look on Wilma's face while she spoke grieved her heart, but she forged on, only hesitating when she reached the part about seeing Kyle slide the bag of drugs into Blake's gym bag.

"I'm sorry, Wilma," Cheryl said, keeping her voice gentle and low. "I know it must hurt to hear this. After all, Kyle is your husband—"

Wilma shook her head furiously, her lips white. "But Blake is my son."

Cheryl held her breath while she waited for her to continue.

"I've put up with a lot the last few years," Wilma said finally. "The loss of our house because of his gambling, our friends." She smiled sadly. "The fights. None of that mattered because I love him." Her jaw clinched, and she lifted her head. "But he's crossed the line this time. I won't let him ruin our son's life the way he's ruined mine."

"What do you mean 'ruined,' Wilma?" Cheryl asked carefully. "What exactly did he do?"

Wilma looked at her dead on then, her eyes cold and hard and surprisingly devoid of tears. "It started at the garage where Kyle worked. Don't ask me how he got mixed up in it. I don't know and don't want to."

"Do you mean drugs?" Cheryl said.

She blew out a breath and nodded. "He said it was because they were cutting his hours, and we needed the extra money. I found out later it was the other way around. They weren't cutting his hours. He just quit showing up for work. When I confronted him, Kyle said it didn't matter. He claimed he could make more money selling drugs on the street than he could ever get working at the garage." Her eyes did fill with tears then, and she blinked quickly to keep them from falling. "Not that it mattered how much he made. Kyle gambled that and then some away. I tried to get him to stop," she whispered, and her hand drifted to the bruise on her arm.

"Blake didn't do that to you, did he?" Cheryl said. "It wasn't really an accident."

Wilma shook her head, her eyes wide and unblinking. "I threatened to leave him after the first time it happened, but he told me he'd take Blake away. He said I'd never see him again."

"So you moved with him, away from Wellington."

"We had to leave. We didn't have any choice. The manager at the garage where Kyle worked threatened to turn him in if he didn't stop bringing drugs around his place."

Cheryl nodded and put her hand on Wilma's knee. "Chief Twitchell needs to know all of this. Will you let me bring him in here, so you can tell us both at once?"

She held her breath, waiting. It was one thing for Wilma to confess to her, but quite another to confess to the police. Would she do it?

"I can't protect him anymore. Not now. Not with him forcing Blake to keep quiet about what he's been doing."

Questions formed in Cheryl's brain, but rather than ask them and make Wilma have to repeat everything in front of the chief, she went to the door and called him in. She briefly summed up what Wilma had told her so far, and then she returned to the sofa and took Wilma's hand.

She ducked her head to look into Wilma's face. "Wilma, what did you mean when you said Kyle was forcing Blake to keep quiet? Do you mean Blake knew about the drugs Kyle put in his bag?"

"No, not that. Blake is totally against drugs. He would never help Kyle sell them." Wilma cast a worried glance at Chief Twitchell. "How much of what I tell you now might hurt my son later on?"

"You should know that everything you say could be used in court," he said, looking at her directly but with compassion mixed in. "If your son was compelled to do something illegal, like aiding a criminal, he will more than likely have to face the consequences."

She shook her head. "That's not fair. Kyle threatened to hurt him. Hurt me, and worse, if Blake didn't do as he was told."

"You'll have a chance to explain all of that to a judge," he said, kindly.

Wilma's gaze shifted to Cheryl. "I can't say anymore. Not until I speak to a lawyer."

"I understand." She took Wilma's hand and gave it a squeeze. "But there is one more thing we need."

Wilma eyed her warily. "What is it?"

Chief Twitchell stepped forward. "Mrs. Dorman, I have reason to suspect that your husband has been selling drugs out of this house. I would like your permission to search the premises."

She shook her head, and Cheryl's stomach sank. She leaned closer. "Wilma, we have to look. Without the drugs, it's just your word against his."

"No, I don't mean that." Wilma stood and looked at the chief, eye to eye. "I mean you won't find any drugs in here, because this isn't where he keeps them."

She smiled then, and it was so surprising that Cheryl forgot to smile back. She simply stared, until Wilma motioned toward the chief's shoes.

"I hope you brought some boots. You're going to need them."

CHAPTER TWENTY-NINE

A contented sigh slipped from Cheryl's lips. It had been a crazy few days since Kyle was arrested, but today was calm...or almost calm. She smiled thinking of Grace's shower earlier that day and the frantic ride to the hospital that ensued when she went into labor midway through. At least all was well that ended well. Baby Ford was healthy and happy and resting comfortably at the hospital with his mother and father when Cheryl left to come home.

A warm breeze stirred the oak leaves over her head, the sound as peaceful as the waves of the Pacific lapping against the coast of Washington.

Cheryl smiled at the memory from her childhood and stirred the swing she sat on with her toe. The Pacific. It had been a long time since she'd visited the ocean. Maybe she and Levi could plan a trip later this summer with little Rebecca. It would be nice to get away for a while, especially now that her mother had called and said that her father's MRI had shown he wouldn't need surgery—just some therapy once his knee was stronger.

She smiled. Of course, that wasn't all she had to be thankful for. Thanks to the drugs Chief Twitchell had found buried in the manure pile, Kyle was now in custody, and Henry was out of it—back at home with his family and hopefully making repairs to their relationship. In fact, this good news meant that they could all go back to their peaceful lives.

She stopped the swing with her foot. Well, not all of them. Wilma and Blake still had a rough road ahead. Wilma had agreed to testify against her husband in exchange for some immunity, but Blake...

She hated to think what difficulties lay ahead for him. At least she could be certain it wasn't drugs she had seen Zach passing to Blake outside of Weaver's. When the chief questioned him about it, he produced a copy of the football practice schedule that he said Zach had given him, a story which Zach later corroborated.

As for the rest? Most of it had yet to be determined. Fortunately, Blake had a good friend in Steven, who had promised to stick by him while the justice system decided what measures they would take, assuming they believed his story and Wilma's about the way Kyle had pressed him into keeping silent.

And Esther?

Cheryl sighed sadly. Chief Twitchell seemed to think she would be assigned community service. Cheryl hoped that was all it would be, since Esther truly had been ignorant of the contents of the bag Zach gave her. Zach, on the other hand, had his own problems to deal with, but with a powerful father and wealthy mother by his side...

Cheryl shook her head and lifted her face to the blue sky. "I'm going to have to trust You with that one," she whispered.

Clouds drifted lazily by, a constant reminder that if God could keep nature in its place, He could certainly order her steps. She smiled.

"Here you are." Levi settled his long form on the swing next to Cheryl. "I've been looking for you."

Cheryl slid sideways and rested her head against her husband's shoulder. "Is Rebecca asleep?"

"Finally." He motioned toward her window. "I left it open a little so we can hear her if she wakes up."

"Thank you."

Levi tucked his arm around Cheryl's shoulders and pressed a kiss to her forehead. "What were you thinking about just now?"

"Esther," Cheryl admitted. "I'll be so glad when all of this is behind her."

"Me too."

He shifted, and Cheryl lifted her face to look at him.

"She and Henry are coming by here in a little bit."

She sat up straight. "What?"

He nodded. "Esther said they both had something they wanted to tell you." Cheryl fidgeted uneasily, and he smiled. "Don't worry. She did not sound angry. I think she wants to apologize."

"You think so?"

"I would be disappointed if I learned it was for something different."

"Hmm." Cheryl resumed her place against his shoulder, but only rested a moment before she sat up straight again. "What about Henry? Won't he be in trouble for lying about the drugs belonging to him?"

"Maybe that is what he is coming to tell you," Levi said.

"Maybe." Cheryl sat back against the swing, but the evening had lost its luster. She couldn't wait to hear what Esther and Henry had to say. "I think I'll go on up to the house and wait for them there."

"Who?"

"Esther and—" She broke off and slapped his knee. "Very funny." She stood. "Are you coming?"

He shook his head. "Ne. I think Esther and Henry would rather speak with you alone." He rose and stretched. "Besides, I'm sure I will hear all about it tonight."

He gave her a kiss and then started for the barn. Poor Levi. Kyle had his faults, but now that he was gone, the work he'd done all fell to Levi.

"Don't work too late," she called.

He waved and continued walking. Cheryl turned for the house. She had barely reached it when a buggy rumbled up the drive. She stopped and waited while Henry climbed out then circled around to assist Esther.

Cheryl met them at the porch and wrapped Henry in a hug. "I am very glad to see you."

"I am glad to be seen."

He rubbed his chin wryly. Though his eyes looked red from lack of sleep, he seemed none the worse for wear. Cheryl motioned them into the kitchen and then crossed to the refrigerator for a pitcher of lemonade.

She set out three glasses and filled them all half full. "So, tell me, Henry, what did the chief say about what happens next for you?"

Henry wrapped his long fingers around the glass as he and Esther sat down at the table and shrugged. "He does not think I will face charges."

"That's good news." Cheryl sat down opposite them.

He nodded. "Ja. I am grateful. For now, it looks like I will get by with a stiff warning."

Cheryl shook her head. "You took such a risk, Henry. You very easily could have ended up spending time in jail. Real time. Not just a couple of days."

He looked at Esther shyly, his cheeks flushed. "It was worth it."

"Was it?" Cheryl said, interrupting the long glance they shared. "What about your parents? They were pretty angry about all of this."

"I will go to them and make my apology," Esther said. "And I will tell them that I intend to do the same thing before the bishop and the church, if he asks it."

She dipped her head and peeked timidly at Cheryl from below her kapp. "That is also why I came here today. I need to apologize to you, Cheryl. I allowed my head to be turned by a boy who is not Amish, and then I pushed you into helping me keep my secret by using your relationship with my brother against you. It is not the same thing. I see that now. I am sorry."

"I accept your apology," Cheryl said, blinking back tears. "Will you be speaking to your parents as well?"

"Right after we leave here," Esther said. Sorrow darkened her brown eyes. "I was very foolish thinking I could resist being tempted when the Scripture clearly warns us against such things. It was my pride that made me think otherwise."

"We are all victims of our own pride from time to time," Henry said softly.

Esther shot him a grateful glance, and something more. Was it admiration? Maybe she was finally starting to see the gentleness and strength in Henry that Cheryl had witnessed all along. She hoped so.

Her phone rang, and while she did not welcome the interruption, it was a number she recognized—Blake. Seeing it reminded her of something else she hadn't understood. She looked at Esther.

"That day the chief came into the store and found the drugs...did you really call Zach?"

Esther nodded. "Zach lost his phone but he told me I could call Blake's number if I needed to get a message to him."

So that was what Blake had given him in exchange for the practice schedule. Cheryl nodded then held up one finger and stood. "Would you guys hang on for just a moment? I need to take this."

Both Henry and Esther nodded, and Cheryl quickly hit the answer button and then ducked into the hall.

"Hello?"

"Cheryl? It's Wilma Dorman."

"Wilma." Cheryl blew out a breath. "I'm glad to hear from you. How are you?"

"Better." Wilma laughed, and it was the first truly happy sound Cheryl had heard her make. "Blake and I are settled in my sister's house in Wellington. She and her husband have two kids of their own, so it's pretty cramped with everyone underfoot, but for now, it's perfect."

"I'm glad to hear that, Wilma."

She sniffed and then came back on the line. "Listen, Cheryl, I'm really sorry. Blake and I talked, and he's agreed to help Levi out on the farm some to make up for everything that happened."

"That's not necessary, Wilma," Cheryl said quickly.

"Thank you. But I really think being around Levi will be good for Blake...that is...if you...I mean..."

"I'm sure we can work something out," Cheryl said.

Wilma sighed in relief. "Well, it might be tricky since we still only have one vehicle, but weekends would work. Blake even offered to drive out on Fridays after school so he could be there early on Saturday."

"What about his football games?"

"He's not interested anymore. He and Steven have been talking about going into mission work. I think Blake wants to reach out to kids who've had problems with drug abuse."

He was really going through with it. Cheryl's eyes stung with tears of gladness. "That's great, Wilma."

"And I might be joining them," she said softly. "There are probably a lot of women who could use some counseling about physical abuse. I'm going to get my own counseling first, but after that...maybe I'll see about starting some kind of ministry."

"I think helping someone else would be the best way you could use what you've gone through."

Wilma was silent for a moment, and then she cleared her throat and said, "I'm really glad we ended up on your farm, even with everything that happened. I don't know that we could have survived all of it otherwise. I just hope, well, I hope you don't regret having us."

Cheryl smiled. "I don't regret it for a minute, Wilma."

"I'm so glad." She sniffed. "Well, I'd better go. I just wanted to thank you one last time and say how sorry I am for everything that happened."

"I'm glad you called. But you will keep in touch, right? And maybe you can come with Blake for the weekend once in a while."

"I will. Thank you, Cheryl. Goodbye."

She hung up, and Cheryl spent a quiet moment thanking God for His protection and goodness, and praying for Wilma and Blake. Maybe now, with Kyle out of the picture, they would finally find their own strength, their own faith. Maybe they could finally build a good life for themselves and others.

Sighing happily, Cheryl returned to the kitchen, and was pleasantly surprised to see Henry and Esther talking, their heads bent together closely. In Henry's eyes, she saw love, and hope, and yearning—all feelings she'd once kept hidden from Levi. Esther, too, looked at Henry with kindness and newfound respect.

Perhaps they might yet make something of those feelings. At the very least, Esther now realized she had a true friend in Henry, one who would always be there for her.

Cheryl smiled and backed out of the kitchen quietly. Truth be told, she wanted more for Henry and Esther than just friendship, but she knew better than to meddle. God's timing was always perfect. She would wait on Him to reveal what, if anything would develop. For now, it was enough to know that He cared for her, for

Levi, for her entire family. And His plan for each of them was good, if only they would learn to wait on Him.

It was a hard lesson, one that Cheryl was finding she would have to learn daily. But she trusted Him.

And that was all that mattered.

Author Letter

Dear Reader,

What a joy it was to be back among friends with this book. I've taken on several projects in the months since my last Sugarcreek Amish Mystery, so I thought it might be difficult. Instead, it was like a meeting with that special person—the one whose friendship resumes right where it left off, no matter how much time has passed.

Cheryl and Levi have experienced many changes. Writing about their adventures chasing after their little one reminded me so much of when my own children were little and what it's like now, chasing after my grandchildren. No wonder the Lord said that children were a heritage from the Lord. They truly are a reward from Him, and it was a joy to write about that blessing for Cheryl and Levi.

The scenes that took place with the youth in this book were familiar as well. I have been an employee at a public school for many years, and a part-time youth director at our church. Writing about the troubles facing teens today was a message from my heart. I hope this story will encourage you to remember our young people in your prayers.

May God richly bless you,
Elizabeth Ludwig

ABOUT THE AUTHOR

Elizabeth Ludwig is an award-winning author whose work has been featured on *Novel Rocket*, *More to Life Magazine*, and *Christian Fiction Online Magazine*. Her first novel, *Where the Truth Lies* (co-authored with Janelle Mowery), earned her the 2008 IWA Writer of the Year Award. This book was followed in 2009 by "I'll be Home for Christmas," part of the Christmas anthology collection *Christmas Homecoming*.

In 2011, her second mystery, *Died in the Wool* (co-authored with Janelle Mowery) was nominated for a Carol Award. In 2012, the Edge of Freedom series released from Bethany House Publishers. Books one and two, *No Safe Harbor* and *Dark Road Home*, respectively, earned 4 Stars from the RT Book Reviews. Book three in the series, *Tide and Tempest*, received top honors with 4½ Stars and was recently named a finalist for the Gayle Wilson Award of Excellence. Elizabeth was also named a finalist in the 2015 Selah Awards for her novella "One Holy Night," part of the best-selling anthology collection, *Christmas Comes to Bethlehem, Maine*. Her latest releases include *Don't Rock the Boat* and *Shifting Sands*, part of the Mysteries of Martha's Vineyard series from Guideposts.

Elizabeth is an accomplished speaker and teacher, often attending conferences and seminars where she lectures on editing for fiction writers, crafting effective novel proposals, and conducting successful editor/agent interviews. Along with her husband and children, she makes her home in the great state of Texas. To learn more, check out ElizabethLudwig.com or visit her on Facebook.

Fun Fact about
the Amish or Sugarcreek, Ohio

Barn raisings, also historically known as barn rearings or raising bees, are events during which a community comes together to build or rebuild a barn for one of its members. In the early years of the American frontier, barns were necessary structures. They provided farmers with storage for crops and hay, and shelter for their animals. But barns were large and costly to build, a feat that was often too much for one man to tackle alone. Barn raisings answered this need, since members of the community were often required to participate. Though they were unpaid, they knew the favor would be returned when they were ready to raise their own barn. And with enough help and a skilled workforce, the task could often be completed in a single day.

By the end of the nineteenth century, barn raisings had become rare in most areas, except for Amish communities, which are still widely known for them. Both an economic and social event, barn raisings are a festive time. The act typifies selflessness and neighbors helping neighbors, two bedrocks of Amish culture.

SOMETHING DELICIOUS FROM
OUR SUGARCREEK FRIENDS

Elizabeth's Cherry Crumble
(This dish is delicious with ice cream!)

Ingredients:

6 tablespoons real
   butter

1⅛ cups all purpose flour

½ cup rolled oats

6 tablespoons brown sugar
   (packed)

1 teaspoon salt

1 can cherry pie filling

Directions:

Heat oven to 375 degrees F (190 degrees C). Melt butter in a large saucepan (be careful not to scorch). Remove from heat and stir in oats, flour, brown sugar, and salt until a dry, crumbly dough forms (do not over mix). Divide into thirds. Press ⅔ of the dough *lightly* into the bottom of a 9 inch square baking pan. Spread cherry pie filling over the crust and sprinkle with remaining crumb mixture. Bake for 40–45 minutes until lightly browned. Serve warm.

Read on for a sneak peek of another exciting book
in the series Sugarcreek Amish Mysteries!

Quilt by Association
by Nancy Mehl

Cheryl Miller looked out the window of the cottage where she'd lived when she first came to Sugarcreek. So many things had changed since then. A tug on the back of her jeans caused her to look down at her seventeen-month-old daughter, Rebecca.

"What is it, Boo Bear?" she asked.

Rebecca put her arms up. "Mama, mama, mama..." she repeated over and over.

Cheryl bent down and picked her up. She nuzzled Rebecca's neck, taking in the aroma of baby shampoo. "I love you," she said.

Rebecca squealed in happiness, but after a few moments of snuggling, she was ready to get down. She wriggled around until Cheryl put her on the floor.

"Don't get into anything," Cheryl told her, as if Rebecca had the ability to control her curiosity.

Levi had moved some of the original furniture back into her aunt Mitzi's house. The cottage was comfortable and charming but still different than when Cheryl lived here. Many of her aunt's personal possessions were now in Cheryl's house. Several people had rented the cottage since Cheryl moved out, but it was empty right now, so it worked out perfectly that an Amish woman from Bird-in-Hand, Pennsylvania was arriving soon to stay for the week. The woman, Sharon Vogel, was bringing some of her homemade quilts to sell in the Swiss Miss. Cheryl had invited her to Sugarcreek so they could talk and so that Cheryl and Esther, who was managing the store now, could see some of her quilts firsthand. Sharon's church had given her permission to ride a bus to Canton, Ohio, where Cheryl's husband Levi, and his mother, Naomi, would pick her up and drive her to Sugarcreek.

Cheryl glanced at the clock. They were running a little late. Cheryl hoped everything was all right. She noticed Rebecca headed for some of Aunt Mitzi's knickknacks on a nearby desk. Keeping Rebecca out of things wasn't easy. She was getting pretty fast. Her little hands could pick up a glass or a cup before her parents had a chance to stop her. As she ran toward the desk, Cheryl grabbed her.

"Where's your dolly?" she asked. She steered Rebecca away from the desk and grabbed the diaper bag. She quickly pulled out the Amish doll Naomi had made for her. *Oma* had a face that Naomi had sewn on. Many people believed all Amish dolls were faceless, but it wasn't true. Many of them had features. Naomi had painted blue eyes on the doll's face and sewn on a red smiling mouth. Rebecca's face lit up, and she put her hands out. Cheryl breathed a sigh of relief. Rebecca would stay busy with Oma for a while. Cheryl thought it was funny that Rebecca named her doll after her grandmother. Truth be told, the doll did look a little bit like Naomi. As Rebecca sat down on the floor with her doll. Cheryl heard a noise from outside and went back to the window. Levi's truck was pulling into the driveway.

Cheryl scooped Rebecca up in her arms and hurried to the front door. She opened it and watched as Levi got out and went around to the passenger side of the truck. Rebecca started laughing and saying, "Dada! Dada!" She certainly was a daddy's girl. She absolutely adored Levi.

Levi helped Sharon out of the truck. Cheryl guessed her to be in her late twenties or early thirties. She was small and very attractive, with a wide smile. She reached up to adjust her prayer *kapp* after a gust of wind swept past her. It was September in Sugarcreek. One of Cheryl's favorite times of the year. The trees were burnished red and gold, but the wind that came with the fall weather could be rough.

Sharon stood to the side while Levi helped his mother out. When she saw Cheryl and Rebecca, Naomi waved and grinned at them. Once she'd smoothed her dress, she put her arm through Sharon's and led her toward the house. Levi went to the back of the truck to get Sharon's suitcases.

When Naomi reached them, she let go of Sharon and reached out for Rebecca who was excited to see her Oma. Cheryl put her in Naomi's arms and turned to Sharon.

"I'm so happy to meet you," she said. "Thank you for coming all this way."

"I am grateful you are willing to look at my quilts."

"As I told you, I saw pictures of a couple of them at a charity auction," Cheryl said. "They were so beautiful. I'd really like to share them with my customers."

Sharon stepped up onto the porch. "I brought three quilts to show you. I'm looking forward to working with you and Esther."

"I am too." Cheryl held the door to the cottage open. "I believe you'll be comfortable here. As I told you, it does have electricity."

Sharon smiled. "Our bishop isn't as strict as some. When we travel or do business, we must accept different circumstances. I am grateful to have such a nice place to stay."

"I told Sharon she was welcome to stay with us," Naomi said, "but that the cottage is so much closer to the store."

"We just want you to be comfortable," Cheryl said.

"I am certain I will be just fine."

Cheryl noticed Levi coming up the walk with three suitcases balanced in his arms. She hurried over and opened the door. He carried the suitcases inside.

"Where do you want these, Sharon?" he asked.

"Perhaps in the bedroom?" she said. "I can unpack them later."

Levi nodded and headed toward the master bedroom.

"Unless you're tired, Sharon, we thought you might like to come to our house for lunch," Cheryl said. "Naomi has done the cooking, so you're in for a treat."

"Thank you," Sharon said. "That would be wonderful. And perhaps on the way back we could stop by a grocery store? I would like to put some food in the house."

"We certainly can," Cheryl said, "but I've already stocked some things I thought you might like. You might want to check out the kitchen first."

Cheryl took her over and showed her what was in the refrigerator and on the shelves.

"This is wonderful," Sharon said. "If it is all right, I would like to buy some oatmeal, some orange juice, and a bottle of chocolate syrup." She blushed. "I must confess that I like a cup of hot chocolate before going to sleep."

Naomi laughed. "I like hot chocolate too, Sharon. We are alike, ain't so?"

Sharon nodded. "It seems we are." She looked at Cheryl. "I can see I will not need anything else. You are very thoughtful."

"We're just happy you're here. Do you need to freshen up before we leave?"

"If you do not mind, I would like that."

Cheryl showed her to the bathroom and then went back into the living room where her husband and mother-in-law waited. "She's very nice," she said. She started to ask them about their trip when her cell phone rang. She took the phone out of her pocket and said, "Hello?"

"It's Chief Twitchell. Uh . . . I need to talk to you. It's important. Can you come by the station?"

Cheryl hesitated. What was this about? "Well, I have a guest from out of town. We're headed over to the shop. Would it be possible to talk to you there?"

There was a long silence, and then Cheryl clearly heard the chief cover the receiver so she couldn't hear what he was saying to someone else. A surge of concern rushed through her. Was something wrong?

Finally, he said, "That would be fine. Will Levi be with you?"

"Yes, he will."

"Good. We'll be there in a few minutes. We'll need to talk to the both of you in private."

"Chief, what's going on? Is everyone okay? Anyone hurt or sick?"

"Everyone is fine as far as I know. This is something different. Let's just talk when I see you."

"It sounds serious," Cheryl said.

He paused again. "It is," he said finally. "We'll explain when we see you." With that, he hung up his phone.

Levi must have noticed her expression. "What's wrong?" he asked.

"I don't know. Chief Twitchell wants to talk to us. He says it's serious. He's meeting me at the shop. And he's bringing someone else." She frowned at her husband. "Do you have any idea what this is about?"

Levi shook his head. "Not a clue. I guess we will find out when we get there."

"I hope everything is all right," Sharon said. "Perhaps you would rather I wait here?"

Cheryl shook her head. "No. Let's keep our plans intact. It's probably nothing." Even as she tried to reassure Sharon, she felt strongly that her comment probably wasn't accurate.

Rebecca began to fuss for her mama, so Naomi held her out for Cheryl to take.

"I am certain it will be okay," Naomi said. "We must not assume the worst."

Cheryl nodded at her mother-in-law. "You're right," she said, but she noticed Naomi's pensive expression.

As they prepared to leave for the Swiss Miss, Cheryl couldn't help but worry. She tried to dismiss the fear that attempted to invade her thoughts, but something told her that unless it was very important, the chief wouldn't have approached them this way. What in the world could it be?

A Note from the Editors

We hope you enjoyed Sugarcreek Amish Mysteries, published by the Books and Inspirational Media Division of Guideposts, a nonprofit organization that touches millions of lives every day through products and services that inspire, encourage, help you grow in your faith, and celebrate God's love.

Thank you for making a difference with your purchase of this book, which helps fund our many outreach programs to military personnel, prisons, hospitals, nursing homes, and educational institutions.

We also create many useful and uplifting online resources. Visit Guideposts.org to read true stories of hope and inspiration, access OurPrayer network, sign up for free newsletters, download free e-books, join our Facebook community, and follow our stimulating blogs.

To learn about other Guideposts publications, including the best-selling devotional *Daily Guideposts*, go to Guideposts.org/Shop, call (800) 932-2145, or write to Guideposts, PO Box 5815, Harlan, Iowa 51593.

Sign up for the Guideposts Fiction Newsletter

and stay up-to-date on the books you love!

You'll get sneak peeks of new releases, recommendations from other Guideposts readers, and special offers just for you . . .

and it's FREE!

Just go to Guideposts.org/Newsletters today to sign up.

Guideposts.®

Visit Guideposts.org/Shop
or call (800) 932-2145

Find more inspiring fiction in these best-loved Guideposts series!

Mysteries of Martha's Vineyard
Come to the shores of this quaint and historic island and dig in to a cozy mystery. When a recent widow inherits a lighthouse just off the coast of Massachusetts, she finds exciting adventures, new friends, and renewed hope.

Tearoom Mysteries
Mix one stately Victorian home, a charming lakeside town in Maine, and two adventurous cousins with a passion for tea and hospitality. Add a large scoop of intriguing mystery and sprinkle generously with faith, family, and friends, and you have the recipe for Tearoom Mysteries.

Sugarcreek Amish Mysteries
Be intrigued by the suspense and joyful "aha!" moments in these delightful stories. Each book in the series brings together two women of vastly different backgrounds and traditions, who realize there's much more to the "simple life" than meets the eye.

Mysteries of Silver Peak
Escape to the historic mining town of Silver Peak, Colorado, and discover how one woman's love of antiques helps her solve mysteries buried deep in the town's checkered past.

Patchwork Mysteries
Discover that life's little mysteries often have a common thread in a series where every novel contains an intriguing whodunit centered around a quilt located in a beautiful New England town.

To learn more about these books, visit Guideposts.org/Shop